Professor Leonardo watched the police search
the room for nonexisting evidence. The detective gestured to the mutilated corpse as he told
a reporter that it must have been suicide—but
Leonardo knew it was murder, even though the
door was found locked from the inside and the
key was in the victim's hand.

Leonardo would solve this seemly unsolvable case—for that is . . .

LEONARDO'S LAW

LEONARDO'S LAW

Warren B. Murphy

PaperJacks LTD.

TORONTO   NEW YORK

PaperJacks

LEONARDO'S LAW

PaperJacks LTD.

330 STEELCASE RD. E., MARKHAM, ONT. L3R 2M1
210 FIFTH AVE., NEW YORK, N.Y. 10010

PaperJacks edition published May 1988

ISBN 0-7701-0822-9
Printed in the USA

CHAPTER ONE

Walton, Connecticut looks like just another one of those nice little towns that line the north shore of Long Island Sound, towns that make it because they are close to New York City, and then try to hide that proximity by decorating themselves with enough Ye Olde Englishe doodads to make the Wife of Bath feel at home.

That's right. Chaucer. Why not? Who says that cops can't read anything besides reports describing "our soich for the poipetrator." And besides, I'm not Irish, not a hundred percent anyway, and I have no kids, not eight, and instead of my wife and I traipsing off to 7 a.m. Mass every Sunday, hand in hand, we don't get along—unless she gets one first, I'm going to get a divorce. What else can I do with a woman whose coffee looks like it ought to be capped and have a derrick built over it? Among other problems.

Back to Walton and its 35,000 souls. Actually, by

Connecticut standards, it's pretty large—particularly considering that the biggest cities in the state, Hartford and Bridgeport, would, either one of them, fit into one ward in Newark, New Jersey. They might not survive, but they'd fit. That accounts for all those stories about Connecticut politicians in Washington turning their backs on "the urban crisis" or "the continuing plight of the cities." It could all be happening on a different planet as far as they're concerned. In politics, as in life, it all depends on whose ox is being gored.

It's not true that half of Walton's 35,000 people are actors and writers and the other half want to be actors and writers—but we do have more than our share of artistic folk. The biggest movie star in the world lives in a house on the bank of the Saugatuck River but the house isn't much and there's always a pickup truck in the driveway and about the most impressive thing about the whole place is a goddam treehouse for his kids that looks like it was designed and built by Frank Lloyd Wright.

He's just one. The town is sprinkled with well-known actors, folk singers, rock stars, novelists, screenwriters, and producers who came to Walton for just the same reasons everybody else has always come to Walton. It's close enough to New York City to be handy, but not so close that you have to breathe the chop suey that passes for air in New York. They all come up here to lead the good life and to blow good grass, and the only pall over this town isn't smog but merely vaporized Acapulco Gold.

The real force in town is old-money Republicans and rising corporate executives on their way to becoming old-money Republicans. They run the town and I guess you could say there was an uneasy truce between them and our arts colony. It works like this: the old guard runs the town and keeps it rich and prosperous and lily white. And the arty people, who spend a lot of time making speeches about equality and brotherhood all around the rest of the country, keep quiet when they come home. They don't participate in the town. That way, if pressed, they can always say they're against what the town's doing. That protects their image. But they don't volunteer any raps against Walton, they don't make any waves, and so things just drift along, peaceful and quiet, with the old, racist Republican money in full charge.

Why not? It keeps the town in pretty good shape. We've got private schools and public schools that are better than the private schools; we've got a good Jesuit college, nice homes, high real-estate taxes, and a relatively honest, if stupid, town administration, and we've got enough work to keep me and my seven-man detective bureau busy. And if the work isn't a lot of double and triple homicides and ax murders and bomb-throwings, so what? Anyway, we've got our own style. We probably lead the nation in rape complaints against delivery boys and trail the nation in actual rapes. This is sometimes described as the bored-wife-whose-husband-works-out-of-town-and-who-changed-her-mind syndrome. And we probably lead the nation in drunk driving, and trail the nation in drunk-driving arrests. This is because we have more alcoholics than any other area in the country, but our police operate on a strict no-partiality principle of don't-arrest-a-drunk-driver-unless-he-runs-amok-in-a-flock-of-nuns-but-just-take-him-home-because-you-never-know-who-he-knows.

I'm not exactly Gideon of Scotland Yard. On the other hand, while it might be dull, I never get shot at. I'll take it, even when it involves wet-nursing a lot of cops who think they're Wyatt Earp, which is what I do best. And most.

I was at my desk in police headquarters, trying not to foul my new seventy-five-dollar sports jacket with the tar and nicotine slicks I carefully deposit on my desk by letting cigarettes burn out. I would use the ashtray but it's always full and whenever I empty it, I set the wastepaper basket on fire. Jim Glennon was out at Benlow High School, taking part in a Career Day program to urge pampered young vandals to become policemen, heaven forbid, and Al Baker, who is the only one of my seven detectives worth the powder to blow him to hell, was out trying to serve a warrant in a nonsupport case. (Another of our major crime categories. We lead the nation in divorces, too.)

I was alone in my office, reading the latest war communique from my intrepid staff, urging me again to ask the town's Board of Selectmen to authorize the police to carry .357 Magnums instead of .38 police specials.

The Board of Selectmen, an august body only slightly smaller than the Army of the Confederacy, is charged with setting town policy. It had turned down the same gun request a month before. It would just be no use explaining to them again that a .357 Magnum wasn't much different from a .38 police special, except it was a better gun, and if the cops were willing to pay for the guns themselves, why not let them carry them? It wouldn't do any good. Dirty Harry had done us in. When Clint Eastwood started making those movies and packing around that .44 Magnum elephant gun of his, he gave all Magnums a bad name. I could spend my life trying to convince the town fathers that a .357 Magnum isn't the same as a .44 Magnum. And my heart wouldn't be in it, anyway.

I had explained this an hour before to Detective Glennon when he handed me the crudely typewritten request. (On a blue detective's report sheet, in violation of standing policy of the Walton Board of Free Selectmen, to wit: "Nothing but official police department reports shall be written on official police department report forms.")

"Jim, have you ever noticed that cops who never fire their guns are the ones who always want bigger guns?"

"No, Lieutenant Jezail," Glennon said. "I never noticed that." Very chilly tone, as if I had questioned his ability to get it up.

"Notice it next time," I said.

"What's wrong with us wanting the best weapons available to protect ourselves and the public?"

"Nothing. Except in this town you could protect

yourself and the public relatively well using a wooden slingshot and inner-tube bands."

"You're on their side, aren't you, Tony?" Glennon asked. This time, the tone was one of hurt. Heart-rending, uncontrollable hurt. I wouldn't have been surprised if he had sobbed.

"Jim, I don't care if you pack a bazooka in a bag. Whatever makes you happy. I just don't think you need it."

"You wait. Some night when one of us has to walk alone, into a dark alley, to go face to face with some nameless faceless criminal, lurking back there in the dark shadows, and we have to go in defenseless because we're unarmed . . ."

"Not exactly unarmed. The police special can blow a door off its hinges," I said.

"A small door. And we walk in there alone, almost unarmed, and one of us is wasted, what'll you do then?"

"Requisition a flag from the property room and give you an inspector's funeral. Twenty-one gun salute."

"Well, I don't want no goddam salute from no goddam .38 police specials," Glennon said. "At least over my broken, bleeding body, you could fire Magnums."

"Jim, you've got my word. I'll do that. I'll fire one myself. I'll hook another one up with a string on the trigger and have the whole goddam Board of Selectmen pull the string. In death, if not in life, they will come to realize you wanted only the best for them. Another martyr to the public welfare."

"Oh, shit," he said.

"Don't forget. You're talking at Benlow High School today about police careers." I checked my watch. "In about twenty minutes."

He nodded his head twice, the first time casually, the second time vigorously as if it were an answer to his first nod. "Right. And I'm going to tell them that this is a fine job, this police work, if you're in a town where the government stands behind you."

"Deliver that line softly, Jim. It's dangerous doing traffic duty on the Post Road. I'd hate to see you hurt."

So after Glennon left, I reread his request and then typed out a formal letter to the Board of Selectmen, urging them to reconsider their decision outlawing the .357 Magnum as an acceptable handgun. Fifteen minutes later I was on my third try at typing it clean and I was almost ready to scrap the whole project.

The selectmen like their letters neat. They're so goddam busy trying to turn this town into an American displacement of Wembley-Tembley on the Thames that I think they'd like their letters illuminated by Capuchin monks and delivered to them by somebody wearing knickers and carrying the note on a red velvet pillow. Making a cop worry about his typing is like convincing Julius Erving that he's got to pay more attention to how he ties his sneakers. It's nonproductive.

A town is a self-sustaining mechanism. If you leave it alone, it'll go on forever. Somehow the tax bills will get sent out and somehow the taxes will be paid and somehow the salary checks will be drawn and cashed and spent and things will just roll along on inertia for years and years until they reach a state of maximum entropy, and by that time, who cares? That is, if you don't tamper with things.

Well, they elect these selectmen by the dozens and the ding-dongs instantly get to thinking they're the Congress of the United States and the new ones fool around for awhile, looking into budgets and doing efficiency studies, and they're good for about three months of that before they realize that no one's going to pay any attention to anything they do or say. Then they stop trying to mess up the orderly chaos that is the normal state of flow of the government.

So, there they are, with nothing to do and all that energy to use up, so they write letters and they promulgate Official Policies On Official Letter Writing and it makes them feel important and Gloryosky, Zero, good all over. And since it does, the people who really operate the government, the bureaucrats and civil service types, pay great attention to all these unimportant manifestos. It's the price we pay to keep the Board of Free Selectmen the hell out of anything they can screw up.

The manifesto I was wrestling with now was the one on letter writing. It was drafted by a retired schoolteacher named Miss Grunt and passed unanimously and it regards a split infinitive as one of the greatest of modern day threats to a free society. The police department, the report said, was one of the major violators of this policy. The actual sentence accusing us of that read this way:

"The Police Department is among the chief violators of this rule, frequently using such phrases as 'to quickly apprehend' in their written reports and letters to the Board of Free Selectmen."

So much for Miss Grunt. Anybody who uses the singular noun police department and then later in the same sentence refers to "*their* written reports" has no way to make me feel guilty.

Anyway, I finally finished the letter without a major strikeover (except where I put an "e" over an "o," and that they would never notice) when the telephone rang.

"Lieutenant Jezail."

It was Doheny, the radio room dispatcher.

"Tony," he said, and there was an unusual crackle to his voice which usually sounded bored from years of talking into a microphone and not making eye contact with the person he was talking to. "Car 21, that's Jackson and McCleary, just called in. There's a death."

"Where?"

"On Brown Farms Road. It's Barry Dawson."

"He's dead?"

"Murdered, they think. Head all bashed in. Jackson and McCleary are there."

"Okay. I'm on my way."

I hung up, sealed my letter to the Board of Free Selectmen in a number-ten envelope, the cheapest kind available, the ones with the glue that tastes like a morning-after mouth, tossed the letter in my out basket, and left the office wondering who might have killed Barry Dawson.

Who, that is, out of 35,000 suspects.

CHAPTER TWO

Brown Farms Road was cut through a vast section of rolling green land that had once been the Brown Farm, a piece of logic inconsistent with the way our town was usually run.

The farm had been carved up now into estates that stretched from the roadway down to Long Island Sound, and the cheapest one of them couldn't be touched by the entire good and welfare fund of all the police credit unions in the state. There were houses that looked like Buckingham Palace and houses that looked like antebellum mansions. One big mother looked like the Firenze Castle and another looked as if Scarlett O'Hara should be sitting on the front porch in a hoop skirt, picking her teeth with Uncle Tom's knuckle bone.

It was Walton's Gold Coast, and a not inconsiderable nugget on it was Barry Dawson's home, a huge

English Tudor sprawl with yellow stucco the exact color of early-season sweet corn.

As I was driving my 1974 black Chevrolet down Brown Farms Road, I guessed that Dawson's death hadn't taken place in the main house.

More likely in his studio, the studio, by the way, being one of the reasons Barry Dawson was hated in Walton.

He was the hometown boy made good who came back to give it to his hometown, but good. He had grown up in Walton, had left after college, and one day he was Barry Dawson, the world's mystery king. He had written a dozen novels, most of them bestsellers, and his literary contribution to America seemed to be the blending together of the conventional mystery and the conventional big sex book. A stroke sleuth.

Anyway. It worked for him. It made him rich and famous and he got a lot of headline space for his string of marriages to strippers and actresses and chorus girls, each one dizzier than the one before, and for his drunken binges and fights in saloons, most of which he lost.

So he had come home and bought the big Tudor mansion and when he was interviewed by the *Walton News*, he announced he was going to make part of it a home for black unwed mothers, "because they don't have a facility like that in Harlem." He was kidding, but in Walton they don't have much of a sense of humor for jokes like that.

He seemed to take pleasure in needling the town. If

we had some kind of bicentennial celebration, he'd open the gates of his estate to a lot of dippy bombthrowers celebrating "Two Hundred Years of Institutional Racism" and "Walton—America's Most Racist Town."

Not exactly your quiet, make-no-waves type of good neighbor.

So Walton bit its lip and waited, and then, about four months back, Dawson applied to the town's zoning commission for permission to build a studio building on his property, where he could work.

The town had been waiting for that and on the night of the hearing, there were two hundred people at the zoning commission, screaming that Dawson's house was in a Class-A residential area, and the zoning laws didn't permit any kind of business building to be erected there, even if it was just a studio for a writer. True, by the way. In most places in Walton, a writer who works in his house is in violation of the zoning laws. If Rodgers and Hart had lived here, they'd be selling shoes. They sure couldn't write music in their homes.

Faced with the law and two hundred people cheering them on, the zoning commission turned down Dawson's application to build his studio.

The town had gotten even. So it thought. But Dawson wasn't about to give up that easily. He got himself a lawyer and they went through the town's laws and ordinances and zoning regulations and they found an obscure, hundred-year-old town ordinance that said that town policy was "to waive zoning laws in all areas where the owner of property wishes to erect, maintain, and operate a free soup kitchen for homeless men and women, the better to bring them to the realization of Christ as Savior."

Don't you know that Dawson jumps into the local paper then with an announcement that he's going to build the building anyway and use it as a free soup kitchen for Bowery derelicts. Well, say this for Walton residents. They know when they're beaten.

So the next week, the zoning commission meets again. There isn't a soul in the audience, and dutifully, they grant Dawson a variance to build the studio on his property where he can work on his books.

Then a couple of weeks after that, there was *The New York Times* interview. Dawson said he was deep at work on his next book. It would involve a rich, racist town in Connecticut where pampered, bored housewives spent most of their time in rut, while their husbands were in New York, martini-ing their brains into mush. The mystery would be that somebody was killing off the town's housewives. Why? the interviewer asked. "Because the killer doesn't like whores," Dawson said. There was more, but that gives the flavor, and of course, faced with a picture of a town so rotten and people so unappealing, everybody in Walton knew that Dawson was going to write a book about them.

I guess on balance I'd have to say that he was not exactly a pillar of our community's life.

I drove past the closed iron gates of the Dawson estate to a dirt road near the property line, and turned in there, heading toward the Sound. Up ahead of me, I saw a police car parked, its nose just short of a tall evergreen. The police car was brown and yellow. Brown and yellow. Christ. But what else in a town that buys Mercedes Benz buses to run its own jitney service?

I nosed in alongside and walked to a cyclone fence gate. The gate was open. It had a neatly printed sign on it.

KEEP OUT, SHMUCK.
BY ORDER OF THE THIRD WORLD
REVOLUTIONARY VANGUARD

Welcome to the wonderful world of Barry Dawson.

He had misspelled "schmuck."

Behind the gate were rock slab steps cut into the hillside, leading down to a hollow in which the Dawson studio was located.

It was a long low building that looked like a chicken barn. The back of the building faced me as I came down the steps. Where the steps ended, a large flagstone walk split off in both directions, surrounding the house and presumably leading to the front door. I saw my two patrolmen, Jackson and McCleary, standing outside one of the windows on the left side of the house.

They were nervous. Every so often, Jackson would lean over to look in through the window, then turn away. McCleary was smoking, and if I were a member of the Board of Free Selectmen he'd get his ass reamed for that because smoking on duty was a no-no. That was outlined in Manifesto Number 276,112

from the Board of Free Selectmen. I lit a cigarette as
I approached them. No point in making McCleary
nervous. He was a young cop and this might have
been his first body.

When they saw me coming, they both tossed salutes,
McCleary's snappy and young, Jackson's a bored old-
timer-to-oldtimer wave. McCleary ditched his cigarette.

"Hiya, Tony," Jackson said.

"What happened?"

"He's in there." He motioned to the window, which
was open all the way from the bottom. One of the
panes of glass had been punched out.

I leaned in through the window, careful not to pick
up in my fingers any of the slivers of glass that had
fallen into the well of the window.

I was leaning into a large room, perhaps twenty
feet square. The walls were paneled in what looked
like a rich, old oak. There was a window on the far
side of the room directly opposite me and another pair
of windows to my right in the middle of the far wall,
behind a huge wooden desk. To the left, there was a
large heavy door, finished in the same oak as the rest
of the room. There was a red-lacquered campaign
chest of drawers against the far wall. Its bottom
drawers were pulled all the way out, and the top
drawers looked as if they had been opened and hur-
riedly closed. In the bottom drawers, I could see piles
of papers.

The floor of the room was decorated with a light
green rug with yellow flowers. It was also decorated

with the body of Barry Dawson. He was lying between me and the door to the room, his feet toward the door, his head toward me. Or, I should say, what was left of his head. His skull had been mashed and his face and hair were matted with blood. Even from the window, I could see that blood had dripped down onto the white short-sleeved shirt and the fringed jeans he had been wearing. He was wearing those leather sandals I always associate with dirty feet.

"We didn't touch anything, Tony," Jackson said.

"You break the window?" I asked.

"Yeah. I went in through the window. He was stiff so I came back out and we called you. We didn't touch anything."

"Good procedure, Al," I said.

He shrugged. "Not just that," he said. "Whole thing looked a little weird to me."

I nodded, and dropped my cigarette into the shrubbery I had priced two weeks before on the Post Road and couldn't afford, then climbed into the room. Jackson followed me but McCleary seemed content to stay outside. He hadn't said a word since I arrived.

"McCleary," I called from inside.

"Yes sir."

"Get up on the horn and get Daniels down here." Daniels was my one-man fingerprint and photograph bureau.

"Yes, sir."

I heard his feet pad away on the flagstone blocks.

"He looks like he's taking it hard," I said.

"We all are," Jackson said. "It's hard not to when the victim was somebody everybody loved so much."

He had a smile across his big ruddy face that somehow didn't seem appropriate in a room where a body was hardening. I looked down at Dawson's body. There was a faint red line leading from it to the door. Probably blood stains, so I knelt down on the other side of his body. Carefully. I didn't want blood on my new jacket. Just out of habit, I felt for the pulse on his right wrist but as soon as I touched the skin, I knew there was no point in waiting for an answering little thump. His skin was chilled. He had been dead for quite a while. Whoever hit him didn't like him much and had a vigorous way of showing it. His head was cleaved open. It reminded me of a guy I'd seen once on a beach in Puerto Rico, scalping coconuts with a machete.

"Who found the body?"

"Telephone man," Jackson said. "He came to talk to Dawson about installing phones. Nobody answered the bell so he started away. Said he didn't know why but he decided to rap on the window as he was walking back to the truck. When he got near the window, he saw the body. So he panicked. He got up into his truck and drove away to find a cop. We were just cruising down the road when he waved us down and told us what happened. We followed him back."

"Where is he now?"

"He was all shook so I let him go to call his office and get some coffee. He'll be back. I got his name and stuff and he'll be back to give a statement."

"Okay." I was still holding Dawson's wrist, I realized, and I quickly let go. I saw something in his clenched hand.

Carefully, I pried open his fingers. His right hand held two things. An old-fashioned brass key, about three inches long, and a little silver tie-tack, about a half-inch square with an engraving of a pen on it, and a diamond inset in the pen.

I picked the key up with my handkerchief. It was shaped like one of those old-fashioned skeleton keys you used to be able to buy in a hardware store for a quarter.

I walked over to the door, careful not to step on any of the red stains on the floor. There were bloodstains on the brass doorknob too. I tried turning the knob with the corner of my handkerchief. The door was locked.

I must have been shaking my head because Jackson said, "What's the matter, Tony?"

"Don't know. This goddam door is locked."

"So what?"

"So I think this is the key to the door. It was in Dawson's hand. Now what the hell is he doing with the key in his hand?"

I looked at Jackson who solved the problem with a shrug. "Who knows?" he said. "Who cares?" is what he meant.

I checked the other windows in the room. They were all locked tight.

"Jackson. This window we climbed in. You sure it was locked when you got here?"

"Yeah, Tony. I tried to open it from the outside. When it wouldn't give, I hammered in that pane of glass with my gun butt and unlocked the window. Then I opened it up and climbed in."

It violated good procedure all to hell but I had to know more about that door. I was still holding the brass key in my hand, inside my handkerchief, so I went over to the door and inserted the key in the lock. Using my ballpoint pen as a lever, I turned the key. I could hear the dead bolt slide open. I removed the key and using the handkerchief I turned the doorknob. It turned easily and when I pulled, the door opened noiselessly on its hinges.

I looked at the side of the door panel at the lock mechanism. It was a brand-new door but an old-time lock. It did not have those buttons you press in to leave a door unlocked or to lock it without using the key.

It was just a heavy dead bolt—the only way to lock the door was with the key. And there was no slot on the other side of the door for a key. I never saw a door like that before; it locked and unlocked only from the inside.

I pulled the door open. The rest of Dawson's studio was one big room. The entire building was a simple, high-ceilinged rectangle. One end of the rectangle had been walled off to create Dawson's office. The rest of the rectangle was one big open living area, the entrance at the far end—a Chinese-looking red-painted door, set into a wall of mostly glass. The sun was starting to dip a little now and it glinted through the window wall into my eyes.

There were panels of stained glass over and on both sides of the main door, the sun passing through them threw colored darts of light on the walls. In the far left corner of the room, a sink and some kitchen cabinets were being put in, and the ceiling over them was still unpainted. A tarpaulin was piled on the floor next to the sink. Dawson's taste in furniture was lousy. Chrome and glass and red fabric. A room like this demanded leather and wood.

I turned back into Dawson's study and walked over to put the key on the desk.

The desk lamp was on.

"Did you turn this lamp on?" I asked Jackson.

"Told you, Tony, I didn't touch anything."

"Okay. I'm sorry."

There was a light tan speaker on the desk, like one of those phone attachments that let everybody in the room hear somebody at the other end make a fool of himself. Which was strange considering there was no phone.

"You know what this speaker's for?" I asked.

Jackson shrugged.

A yellow legal-sized pad was on the desk with writing on it. A Bic ballpoint pen lay on the pad and, for a moment, I thought that Dawson might have written down the name of his killer. No such luck. It was poetry or something. It had yesterday's date at the top of the page and then some kind of nonsense about the sun turning dull brown dirt into flowering bright life and dagger-jagging flashes of light transforming oak into tiny farms and then the sun dies. It was real puke. I write better poetry than that.

I turned off the lamp by pulling on the little chain that hung from the green plastic globe that covered the two bulbs.

"So what's the big deal with the door?" Jackson asked.

"The big deal is that the door was locked from the inside. And Dawson had the key in his hand."

"So?"

"So how the hell did the killer get out of this room?"

"He dematerialized. They do it on 'Star Trek' all the time," Jackson said. He was never going to make a detective.

CHAPTER THREE

The word phlegmatic doesn't begin to capture the genius of Waldo Semple, the peerless leader of Walton's finest; "just another of the boys in blue who got a break and rose to the top of the heap," as he reminded us each year at the annual police department communion breakfast.

No, phlegmatic wouldn't do. Comatose? Perhaps. Unconscious? It gets close. Ah, yes. The walking dead. That was Chief Waldo Semple.

Semple had been on the force for forty years, joining up back in the Depression days before Walton became an in colony for New York expatriates and commuters. The Board of Free Selectmen had appointed him as chief five years before, apparently on the highly commendable theory that rewarding seniority—Semple was the senior man on the force—would show the other animals in the department that they, too, could rise to the top of the heap if they kept their noses clean and to the grindstone and up in the air sniffing the wind and stopped trying to shoot the town up with nine-thousand caliber Magnums.

Semple's appointment always seemed to me less than an endorsement of seniority. But I was prejudiced, I guess. I have this lingering bias that keeps telling me that police chiefs ought to be alive.

Semple's character, what there was of it, had been stamped, no doubt, by the same sort of genes that had given him his unusual physical beauty. He was a short and stocky man with a head that was totally bald except for a few random hairs that grew above each ear and that he seemed to regard as malefactors. He was constantly rubbing with the fingertips of both hands, stroking them toward the back of his head, hard, as if he were trying to wear them down, rub them out, and eliminate all traces of their having existed. His face seemed almost featureless. Oh, sure, he had the normal requirements of eyes and ears and nose and mouth, but each was so ponderously nondescript that the impression one got of Chief Semple was that of a flesh-colored artillery shell, wearing an ill-fitting brown suit.

He had learned his police work by surviving, which means to say that he knew pretty damn little, because the amount of police skills you pick up are in direct proportion to your willingness to take chances, to risk making mistakes. He supplemented these meager skills by reading detective novels of crime and violence in the big city and he talked like a vice-squad cop in a pornographic police story.

So much for the good things about him. The other side of the coin is that Chief Semple was crass, bigoted, suspicious, narrow-minded, and stupid to the point where I believed he would be happiest sitting on the ground behind a picket fence, spending his days catching and eating worms.

He did not like me. He thought I was a wise-ass troublemaker. Oh well, even a stopped clock is right twice a day.

When the chief arrived on the scene at Barry Dawson's, he did his usual level best to solve everything for us immediately.

"Anybody see a nigger skulking around?" he said. "Niggers do this kind of thing."

Walton had six black families. Two doctors, a lawyer, an engineer and two New York bankers. Their average income in thousands was higher than Chief Semple's IQ in units. It didn't matter. He was still convinced that they were behind all the crime in town.

I didn't answer him. I was busy showing Daniels, my photo and print man, what I wanted him to shoot. As the highest-ranking officer in the room, it was my responsibility to respond to the chief so he cleared his throat ominously toward my back, and repeated:

"I said, anybody see any niggers around here?"

Daniels underway, I answered, "No, Chief. Not a one."

"Have your men check the neighborhood. Ask if anybody saw any niggers."

"They're checking now, Chief. Baker and Waldron

are out." What neighborhood? I wanted to ask. The nearest house was half a mile away.

"They gonna ask about niggers?" Chief Semple asked, as if, unless he were asked specifically, some neighbor might forget seeing a seven-foot black man, dressed in a loin cloth, wearing a bone in his nose, walking up to Dawson's house, carrying a voodoo drum and a ballpeen hammer.

"They're going to ask about everybody," I said mildly.

The chief's eyes narrowed suspiciously as if I were joined with the rest of the world in a plot to keep homicidal Africans out of jail. But he didn't say anything, except to mumble, "Look for a nigger."

It annoyed me to hear him keep using that offensive word. He was like a fifty-year-old Irish barfly who's just found out he can swear in the presence of the woman sitting next to him without getting rapped on the knuckles by Sister Mary Leviathan, and so proceeds to divest himself of as many fucks, bastards, pricks and cunts as he can fit into each sentence. Strange what gives some people their feeling of power and how tenuous that feeling is. I once saw Chief Semple meet a black official of the Justice Department. He did everything but shine the man's shoes and offer to run out and buy him a watermelon or take him to tap-dancing school. He sweated the whole meeting.

I watched Daniels take photos while the chief sat behind Dawson's desk at the far end of the room and began to pooch around the desk, thus probably destroying whatever clues might have been there.

And right about that time, a clue wouldn't have hurt.

"Jezail," the chief yelled.

"Right, Chief."

"Brief me." I turned around. Semple's tiny, pinprick eyes were coursing the room, looking at the other four policemen there, making sure they had observed who was the ranking power in the room.

I sat in a chair alongside the desk.

"This is the way we found everything. The dresser drawers pulled out. All the windows closed and locked. The desk neat. The lamp on."

The asshole had started doodling on Barry Dawson's yellow legal pad! I took it away from him, tore off the top sheet, folded it and put it in my pocket.

"The body hasn't been moved. When the doc comes we can be sure, but the side of his head was bashed in and that looks like it to me. There's a trail of blood between the body and the door. The door was locked from the inside. It only locks with a key and Dawson had the key in his hand."

"What key?" Semple said.

"The one you're fingering now, getting your prints on," I said. The chief dropped the key onto the desk blotter but glowered at me.

I looked around the room to refresh my memory. "The body was found by a telephone installer who looked through the window and saw Dawson on the floor. Jackson broke a window to get in. The body was cold so I don't know how long he had been dead. The doc again. Dawson had that key. I said that. He also had this."

I took a small glassine envelope holding the tie-tack from my jacket pocket and put it on the desk in front of Semple. He picked it up and peered closely at it, as if there were a millimeter-sized informant on it, signalling the solution to him with microscopic semaphore flags. Satisfied that there wasn't, he looked back at me and dropped the tie-tack on the desk.

"Daniels has dusted for prints. There were some on that open chest of drawers but they look like old ones. We'll check more after the doc gets here. We don't know if anything's missing. The dresser's just got papers in it. Old manuscripts and things. Nobody is up at the main house, so we haven't been able to question his wife or whoever else lives up there."

"What about a murder weapon?" Semple asked.

"No sign of one. I checked all the things in the room that might bat somebody's head in and they're all clean. No bloodstains, nothing."

"How the hell can there be a murder without a murder weapon?" the chief asked with, for him, a high degree of common sense. "And you say the room was locked from the inside? How the hell can that be?"

I shrugged. "I don't know," I admitted. "Must be one damn smart nigger murderer out there, probably poised to strike again."

Behind me, I heard Daniels cough to cover his

laugh. I picked up the tie-tack before the chief lost it and put it back in my pocket.

When the telephone installer came back, I had one of my men take a statement from him and then, to calm his nerves, I had him install a temporary telephone in Dawson's office for us to use.

So Chief Semple was on the telephone with his wife, telling her about the exciting case he was working on, when Doctor Spears arrived. Spears was a pleasantly efficient man who got paid the magnificent sum of $2,500 a year for being the town's medical examiner and who treated each of the dozens of cases he handled each year as if it and it alone were producing that $2,500 fee. He carefully examined Dawson's body, unbuttoning and rebuttoning his clothes, noting the condition of the flesh, occasionally mumbling to himself. Then he stood up and came over to where I was looking through the chest of drawers that had been ransacked.

"Tony," he said.

"I'll take that report, Doc," bellowed the chief who had finally finished titillating his wife.

Doc Spears ignored him.

"There's no marks on the body except that head wound," he told me.

"What's that?" Semple yelled.

"He says there's no marks on the body except the head wound," I called back. "When do you think he died?"

"Yesterday, some time," Spears said. "I'll know better after an autopsy."

"And it was the blow on the head?"

"What's that, Jezail?" the chief yelled.

"Trying to find out what killed him, Chief," I said.

"Oh."

"Yes," Spears said. "You haven't found the weapon?"

I shook my head. "You make anything of those bloodstains?"

"That's tricky. They've been smeared. It looks like he crawled from the door to where he died," Spears said.

"Just a guess, Doc. If . . ."

"What are you talking about, Jezail?" the chief yelled. I raised a hand for silence, ignored him and continued.

"If he got socked on the head that hard, would he have lived long enough to crawl back from the door?"

"Sure. He could have. He could have lived seconds. Minutes. The skull is bashed in but you can never tell how fast somebody will die from any given wound."

He looked at the expression on my face and said, "Doesn't help, huh?"

"I don't know. There are too many questions. Why would he crawl away from the door when the door was the way out?"

"Maybe trying to get to a phone?" Spears said.

"No phone."

"Head smacked up, he might not have remembered that."

I nodded. "Doc, he had the key in his hand when we found him. He locked the frigging door himself."

It was his turn to shake his head. "That doesn't make any sense."

"Well, it's either that . . . or the killer vanished from a locked room," I said.

"Hah?" called the chief. "What's going on?"

"The doctor was just saying the case doesn't make too much sense."

"Well, we know that. For Christ's sake," the chief said.

While the doctor was cleaning up, I gave my men instructions on what to do, and then I walked out with Doc Spears.

As I passed the broken window of Dawson's studio, Chief Semple saw me and hollered: "Jezail. Where are you going?"

"Got to think for a while," I said reluctantly.

"I don't want you going near that fag."

But I was already past the window and pretended I hadn't heard.

CHAPTER FOUR

"That fag."

The kind of man who could call Professor Leonardo "that fag" could call Paderewski a Polack piano player or Einstein a tricky Jew accountant.

Really. Sometimes I couldn't understand how Chief Waldo Semple got up the nerve to leave his house in the morning.

Misericordia College is a Jesuit school that sits on sixty wooded acres in the southwest corner of Walton, the corner nearest New York City. I suspect that Jesuit schools attract a better type of clientele than do secular colleges. At least, that's the feeling I get every time I drive into Misericordia off Route 136, a narrow two-lane road for which the title "route" is an undeserved compliment.

The Misericordia grounds are always green and mowed and clean and litter-free. The students wear, what else, jeans and tee shirts, but they somehow seem cleaner than the same clothes worn by some bebopper at N.Y.U., majoring in homemade nuclear weapons. Maybe it has something to do with their being Catholics. I never see a sloppy monsignor.

I think they missed the boat when they built the college in the fifties, right after the Korean War. I've got this weak spot for church architecture and I think a Catholic school would be a great place to let it all hang out. Great vaulting ceilings. Turrets. Spires. Belfries.

So what'd they build? Twelve buildings that looked like garden apartments. *3½ rms w vue. Pool, suitable for baptisms, tennis on site. $410 with all utilities including God. Off street parking.*

When I arrived at the school, I headed for Leonardo's lecture room, which was in the science building, on the main floor at the end of the corridor, poured cement covered with green indoor-outdoor carpeting. Ptaah for American college architecture.

There was a neat black and white nameplate screwed to the wooden door.

DEPARTMENT OF MATHEMATICS
Dr. David Vincent Leonardo
Professor

The door opened into the back of a classroom. Like all of Leonardo's classes, it was filled up. Eighty little wooden chair-desks in neat Catholic rows and files. There was one empty seat across the room, but before I could move toward it, a young man in the seat nearest the door nodded to me and got up to give me his seat. I raised a hand in mild protest but he just nodded again, got up and went to the empty seat across the room. The woman he sat down next to was stunning.

Ah well, some things are Catholic and some things are catholic. I was happy at least that he hadn't been in a hurry to seat me because I looked like I couldn't be trusted to stand without aid. I'm only forty-five.

Leonardo was standing alongside his desk at the other end of the classroom, his back to the students, looking for something in one of his desk drawers. Near his desk was a large rolling blackboard, the kind that went out of style in the public schools, along with education. Except where a blackboard had slate, this one had a sheet of clear plexiglass. Leonardo usually stood behind it, looking through the glass at the class. And when he wrote on it, he wrote backwards so that the students, on the other side of the plexiglass, could read it like regular left-to-right writing.

Leonardo turned back toward the class, a small smile on his face, the face that set a lot of hearts fluttering in Walton. I mean, the man could have been a movie star, he was so good-looking. When he first came to town, the women went bananas and then, right away, some started passing rumors that he was a queer.

Well, you didn't have to be a detective to see what had happened. Leonardo had said no to them and they had to accept one of two alternatives. Either he wasn't attracted to them or he was a flaming pervert. Guess which one they picked.

The second week he was in town, that rumor was in

full bloom but it wilted kind of quickly when this movie actress visited him for a weekend. Somebody said something to her about Leonardo's abnormal sexual preferences and the actress gave a deep roaring laugh that must have taken the skin off the woman who passed the remark.

That was the end of the talk about Leonardo's homosexuality. Looking at him though, this morning, I could understand how a rumor like that could have gotten started. The man was something to look at. I knew he was thirty-five but he looked twenty-five. He had this soft curly black hair and an unwrinkled tan complexion. He looked like a Mediterranean lifeguard and he had the build of one, a V from the wide shoulders to the narrow waist, with the smooth movements of a champion gymnast.

He wore metal frame glasses, usually pushed up on top of his head, and once he had confided to me that the glasses weren't for anything, except to make him look older and more scholarly. Women thought they made him look sexy.

He needed scholarly like I needed another bill to pay. Three years earlier, when he first came to Misericordia, the college had planned a festival of the arts and sciences. Symposiums, lectures, art displays, the whole thing. I guess it was rigged up somehow to some kind of fund-raising program.

Anyway, don't you know that just before the festival was supposed to open, the faculty came down with the flu. All but Leonardo. So what'd he do? He ran the whole thing himself. He chaired panels on art, science, physics, literature, environment, you name it, he did it. I wouldn't be surprised if he parked guests' cars too. *The New York Times* covered it and called it "a dazzling display of scholarship and genius." Kind of a Jim Thorpe of the intellect, a one-man team.

This is the man my peerless leader calls "that fag."

Leonardo had been looking for a grease pencil in the desk. He had it now and walked back to the plexiglass "slate." He looked through it, around the room, but apparently didn't notice me because he did not react.

"The beauty of numbers does not lie in their symmetry," he said, "even though their symmetry is beautiful. It does not lie in their precision, even though their precision is beautiful. The beauty of numbers lies in their utility."

He started to write on the plexiglass. That man could write faster backwards than I could forward, his left hand just seeming to fly over the surface, but his letters and figures precisely carved, as if made by a professional calligrapher. He put on the glass something that looked to me like this:

$$Wm \text{ equals } \frac{a^m}{m!} e^{-a}$$

That, I was to find out in the next ten minutes, was something called the Poisson Distribution, which you could use to predict with accuracy the number of cavalry soldiers kicked to death by horses in a year, the number of fatal dogbites in New York City, the possibility of a run on rattlesnake meat at your local food market, even the number of wars in the world in the next five years.

I also learned about the Fibonnacci series, the difference between ziggurats and pyramids, the interesting fact that on a map, Upper Egypt is in the lower part of Egypt and vice versa. I learned that stillborns mummify and need no embalming, that flies are born full grown, that many Peruvians bear the Mongolian Spot birthmark, and that albinism is as frequent among blacks as among whites.

And all the while this was going on, there wasn't a sound in the room except for Leonardo's softly musical voice. The students did not miss a word. He spoke softly, without contractions, as if he had learned English from a phonograph record.

What Leonardo was getting to, as best as my non-Jesuitical mind can figure, was the interlocking universality of knowledge. That all disciplines are important and scholars should not discard information from any field, because one never knows its potential application. But when there are too many pieces of information, too many variables, problems may become just too unwieldy for any one mind to solve, and then mathematics is necessary to unlock the mysteries and to solve the riddles.

It was quite a performance. It was even more impressive when I remembered that this was mathematics and Leonardo could have done the same thing in a half-dozen different fields without blinking an eye.

When Leonardo stopped, a young man got quickly to his feet and said he had a problem.

"Which is?" asked Leonardo.

"Earlier today in methodology, we were all given a problem to solve. The idea was to figure out how we attacked problems and tried to find solutions. We thought . . ." He paused and looked around at the rest of the class. "We thought it might be interesting to give you the problem."

"Yes. It would be interesting," Leonardo said.

"We're not interested just in a solution, but in the method of solving it, too," the student said.

"I understand," Leonardo said. There was a faint smile on his lips.

"Perhaps I ought to warn you. The best time for solution in methodology class was four minutes and twelve seconds," the student said.

"Which was, of course, your time," Leonardo said. The class laughed and the student blushed and nodded.

"The problem," Leonardo said.

"This is it. What is the sum of all the numbers from one to one hundred?"

Leonardo nodded, then looked off into space. Those large black eyes seemed to glisten. If I had met him on the street and he had looked that intense, I would have been afraid for my life. He stared ceilingward for no more than five seconds, then tapped three times on the plexiglass with the grease pencil he still held in his left hand.

He began to write. As he wrote, he spoke.

"Let X equal the largest integer in a series of X consecutive integers. Then the sum of all the numbers from one throught X will be X times ½ X plus ½ X.

"In the series you gave me, X is one hundred. So the sum of the numbers from one through one hundred is X, one hundred, times ½ X, or fifty, plus ½ X, another fifty. One hundred times fifty plus fifty. Five thousand and fifty.

"If the limiting number, if X, had been ninety-nine, the answer would be ninety-nine, X, times forty-nine point five, ½ X, plus another forty-nine point five, ½ X. That is four thousand nine hundred fifty."

He stopped speaking and flickered a smile at the student who still stood, watching Leonardo write the formula on the plexiglass.

"Another of Leonardo's Laws," he said. "For your collection."

The classroom applauded. I mean, really applauded. Now I know Leonardo is something else, but, still, who'd believe math students applauding a professor for solving a problem? In this day and age?

"How did you do that?" the student asked. "Not just the answer but a formula. How?"

"Someone once asked Newton how he was able to discover the principles of the universe," Leonardo said. "Newton answered, *Nocte dieque incubando*. By thinking about it day and night. That is how I solved it."

The student still looked confused. "Day and night? I just gave you the problem."

"My days and nights pass very quickly," Leonardo

said. "And now you will have to excuse me. My good friend, Lieutenant Jezail of the Walton Police has come to see me, and since he has not fallen asleep during this dull lecture, I suspect this is a business call, not a social one."

"We'll go bail, Professor, if you need it," one student called. The rest laughed.

Leonardo said, "Let us hope it does not come to that." He grabbed a black cardigan sweater, looped it over his shoulders and followed me out into the hall. Telling him that I wanted him to look into a case was like ringing a bell in front of one of Pavlov's dogs. He could hardly be restrained, but I restrained him enough to let me drive us back to the Dawson studio. I'd driven with Leonardo before. He has this immaculately restored 1937 Cord and he drives as if he's spent his life giving A.J. Foyt lessons in cornering at speed.

In the car, on the way back to Brown Farms Road, I told Leonardo about Dawson's curious death. He listened quietly and if I hadn't known better, I would have thought he wasn't paying attention because those bright black eyes flashed back and forth, to the left and right, then focused ahead of us. Then he turned to look behind us. It wasn't that he was looking for something or at something in particular. It was just one of his disconcerting habits; being interested in everything at the same time.

I began to slow up to pay the quarter toll at the booth on the Connecticut Turnpike and began to pull into the left lane where you just dump your quarter in a hopper, get an electronic thank you from a red light that turns green, and go ahead.

"Get to the right, Anthony," Leonardo said. "It will be faster."

"No, it won't. This lane's for exact change."

"The right lanes will be quicker. Did you never notice that drivers approaching these booths form half a Gaussian curve? Highest at the left, lowest at the right."

I allowed as how I had never noticed cars forming half a Gaussian curve at toll booths, but I pulled to the right anyway and when I got to the booth it was empty, and I gave my quarter to the toll collector and sped through.

As I was getting off at the exit, I asked Leonardo:

"So what do you think?"

"A very interesting murder," he said.

"Murder? Just like that? No suicide?"

"One cannot commit suicide without an instrument," he said. "His head was beaten in, but there was no instrument."

"None at all."

"Did you look in the fireplace?"

"There isn't one in the room."

"Is there a chimney of any kind?"

"No."

"All right. With no instrument, it was murder."

"But the door locked from the inside. The key in Dawson's hand."

"Details," Leonardo said. "One thing at a time. There are four ways people can die. Accident, natural

causes, suicide, or murder. Accident and natural causes
are eliminated. Suicide is eliminated because there was
no weapon for suicide. What is left is murder. Now it
may be an unusual murder. It may be a clever murder.
It may even be a brilliantly conceived, incredibly well-
executed murder. It could be those things, but one
thing it definitely is, is murder."

"Reminds me of something I read once in Sherlock
Holmes," I said.

"Yes?"

"When you have exhausted all the other possibilities, the one remaining, no matter how unlikely, must
be the truth. Something like that."

"Yes. Well, that is correct," Leonardo said. He
sounded almost grudging.

"Sherlock was pretty shrewd," I said.

"He was an idiot," Leonardo said sharply. "I remember . . ." His voice stopped abruptly in mid-
sentence. I waited but he said nothing more.

"Yeah?" I said. "You remember . . . ?"

"Nothing," he said, and he was silent until we got
to Dawson's studio.

Speaking of idiots, there was a press car parked on
the hill overlooking the studio when we got there. It
had "Channel Ten News: Your Eye On Connecticut"
written on the side.

That would mean, more than likely, Cletis Johnson,
a big, black incompetent, with a mouth of mush and a
plan to make it to the big time in New York by proving he was too nasty for Connecticut.

And still speaking of idiots, Chief Semple was talking to Cletis Johnson in front of the main door to the house. Semple had his hands jammed into his jacket pockets and his jaw pushed forward. Johnson, fully half-a-head taller, kept jabbing a microphone toward Semple's mouth as if it were a barbecue fork and the chief was a hot dog starting to roll off a backyard grill.

Behind them, facing them and us, was a cameraman with a portable rig, whirring away at Semple's face.

"Interesting specimens," Leonardo murmured.

Chief Semple looked to his left and saw me coming.

"There he is," he said to Cletis Johnson. "Jezail, come talk to this guy, will you? And then I want to see you." He tried to make his voice sound ominous, but only succeeded in sounding ridiculous. Without waiting, he walked back inside the house.

Johnson tried to impale me on his microphone but I caught the top of it in my hand and held it, and met him eye to eye.

"What did the chief tell you, Johnson?"

"Nothing. I don't get to Walton too much but every time I do, I have trouble with you people. Let go of my microphone."

"Not just yet," I said. I noticed Leonardo walking back along the flagstone path, head down, looking.

"You know who's dead?" I asked.

"Right. Barry Dawson. So is it murder or suicide?"

Oh, what the hell, I thought. "Murder."

"Hey, good. Now we're getting somewhere." He

tried to pull the microphone from my hand. I squeezed it tighter.

"Look, Johnson. Let's try to get along. You've got your shots of the house?"

He nodded.

"Okay. I'm going to post a cop up at the top of the hill steps to keep other reporters away, so you've got the best stuff going in. Now I'll let go of the microphone, you ask me your usual three questions, I'll answer them, and then you get out of here and we'll have a press conference at police headquarters at four o'clock or so. Okay?"

"You mean I can't go inside and shoot?"

"That's what I mean. We can't take a chance on mucking up any evidence with people traipsing around."

He snickered. The big son-of-a-bitch snickered. But I waited and he nodded, so I let go of the microphone.

Johnson nodded to his cameraman and I heard the faint whir of the TV camera start again. I wondered how my new jacket would photograph. I was glad it was a subdued pattern. It always jars me when I watch television and there's some kind of bloody triple ax murder and the detective on camera is dressed like he just came off the beach at Waikiki.

"What's your name?" Johnson asked.

"Lieutenant Anthony Jezail. J-E-Z-A-I-L. Detective commander."

He nodded. "Okay." He lowered his voice from B flat to G. "Lieutenant Jezail, what happened here?"

"Shortly before noon today, the body of Barry

Dawson, the famous author, was found on the floor of his office-studio on his estate. The body was discovered by a telephone installation man who had come to the studio to hook up telephones for Mr. Dawson."

"What was the cause of death?"

"The medical examiner has made a preliminary judgment that death was caused by a fractured skull, the result of a severe blow or blows to the head. He had apparently been dead a number of hours."

"So this is murder?"

"Yes. It appears so."

"Do you have any suspects?" That was four questions.

"Not at this moment, but our investigation is just beginning."

I held up my left hand, the one away from the camera, and raised four fingers. Four questions. That was all.

"You'll have to excuse me now, Mr. Johnson. The press conference will be later this afternoon."

He motioned his cameraman to stop shooting.

"You can find your way back up?" I said pleasantly.

"All right. Four o'clock," Johnson said. He made it sound like a threat. He had obviously been talking to Chief Semple too long.

So much for Johnson. Things were bad enough right now that I didn't need a gaggle of reporters hanging around pestering us about a murder mystery. That would happen soon enough.

When I went into the house, the door was slightly ajar and Chief Semple was standing behind it. He had been listening to my interview. I'm glad I hadn't used curse words; he might have been breathing hard.

"Jezail, why did you tell him it was murder?" he demanded.

" 'Cause it was."

"Jesus Christ, we don't need no murders in this town."

That struck me as a strange thing to say. Maybe there was a Board of Free Selectmen manifesto against murders, which I hadn't read.

"Well, we've got one now."

"And why did you bring him?"

"Him" was Leonardo. He apparently had been promoted from "that fag."

"Because I thought he might help. He's helped us before."

"He helped *you* before. I don't need no help from no fag."

"Good afternoon, Chief. It is nice to see you again." Leonardo's musical voice came from the open door behind us.

"Yeah," Semple growled. "Good afternoon. What's good about it?"

The chief stomped away and when I looked at Leonardo, he smiled and shrugged.

There was an old man waiting just inside the house. He was leaning against the sink, smoking a cigarette with deliberate, slow puffs. He wore bib overalls, made of that thick denim that lightens the more you wash it, but never seems to thin out. The man's face was leathered, thin lines map-tracking across it, with the look of creases in a well-used billfold. He looked up as Leonardo and I came into the house, seemed to take our measure, then looked away.

It took me a moment before I placed him. Gunter Wilke. Wilke and Son, Builders. Around town, he was considered the Tiffany of wood. If you wanted the Taj Mahal built of mahogany, he'd be your man. I couldn't believe that he was at Dawson's to put in a kitchen.

Leonardo had already walked away from me toward Wilke. I heard him say:

"Guten tag."

Wilke looked up and answered in German. Leonardo spoke again and Wilke answered again.

"Mr. Wilke," I said. "I'm Lieutenant Jezail. Are you the man putting in this kitchen?"

I must have touched a nerve, because he was kind of huffy. "I build the house, I build the kitchen," he said. That was it. He had built the whole place.

"I suppose you know what's happened here."

"Yeah," he said. It sounded like "ja." The scribbler has been killed."

"Were you working here yesterday?" I asked.

"The kitchen is not finished," he said. "I work until it is finished."

"Yesterday?" I asked again.

"Ja," he said.

"I was wondering if you could shed any light on Mr. Dawson's death for us."

"I am a builder, not a detective," he said. He returned to puffing his cigarette. Why is it foreigners are always so distrustful of police?

"Yes, of course. When did you see Mr. Dawson last?"

"Yesterday afternoon. I work in here. It gets late. I say good night and I go home."

"And where was Mr. Dawson when you said good night?"

"He was in his office."

"Was he doing anything?"

"Yes. Standing at the door."

Gunter Wilke was becoming annoying.

"You worked here all day?"

"Ja."

"Did Mr. Dawson have any visitors during the day?"

"I did not see any."

"Did he say anything during the day, anything that might indicate what happened to him last night?"

"He said nothing during the day."

"Nothing at all?"

"Lieutenant, Mr. Dawson hires me to build this building for him. I work for him before. He asks me if I know what he does for a living. I tell him, yes, I know he writes dirty books. We do not talk much after that. I build the house and then he says I don't like the kitchen, change the kitchen, so I change the kitchen after he pays me first."

"So you were here all day and Dawson was here all day."

"He was here when I came. He was here when I

left. Only time I leave is to go eat lunch on the beach. I always eat lunch on the beach."

"And he had no visitors?"

"Correct."

"And he did not speak to you?"

"Correct."

"He spent the day writing?"

"He was in his office. The door was closed most of the day."

"And what time did you leave?"

"When it was too dark to work anymore."

"And Mr. Dawson was alive then?"

"He opened his door to say good night to me. He was alive enough to do that."

"All right," I said. "One of our detectives will take a statement from you."

I started to turn away but I was stopped by a slow smile, almost a triumphant smirk, on Gunter Wilke's face. It was as if something I had said confirmed a long-held suspicion of his.

"You're not going to ask me about my tool box?" he said. Oh, I hated that man immediately.

"Yes. What about your tool box?"

He pointed to the box at his feet. "My claw hammer is missing. I put it there last night when I finished work. It is not there today."

I nodded and looked at Leonardo. Doctor Spears's murder weapon.

"Thank you," I told Wilke.

There were half a dozen policemen around the house wasting the taxpayers' money, but drawn to the scene of a killing like an arsonist to a tenement fire. I put them to work looking around the house for the hammer and warned them that if they found it, not to pick it up because there might be prints on it.

Behind me, I heard Leonardo still talking to Wilke, this time, mercifully, in English. I hate German as a language. It seems somehow indecent that man has spent millions of years raising himself up from ape-hood by virtue of an intellect and an articulated, opposed thumb, and then should celebrate by talking in grunts.

They were talking about Barry Dawson's books.

"You do not like them?" Leonardo said questioningly.

"Incorrect. I like them. They are entertainments. They are not logical puzzles." As I turned back, he had paused and was staring hard at Leonardo. "You are that Doctor Leonardo, aren't you?"

"Yes."

"I have heard of you," Wilke said.

"Anything good?" Leonardo said, smiling.

"No."

"You have the advantage over me. I know nothing about you," Leonardo said.

"I know," said Wilke.

Patrolman Arthur Cantabile found the hammer, a feat that he celebrated by yelling a lot, lest someone else get credit for it.

When I got outside, I saw Cantabile in the bushes alongside the flagstone path that led from the studio to a fence, behind which the main Dawson house sat, some two hundred yards away. The hammer was resting in some shrubbery about five feet off the flagstone walk.

"Hey, hey, lieutenant, I found it," Cantabile yelled. He pointed into the bushes. "I found it. Here it is. The hammer, Lieutenant. I found it."

"All right, Cantabile, I heard you. Stop the screaming before the chief gets upset."

"I heard that, Jezail." Chief Semple's voice was behind me. "Be careful with that hammer. Don't mess up any fingerprints on it. You wouldn't want to mess up any fingerprints that are on it. Better not touch it until Daniels gets here."

"Cantabile," I said. "You stay here and make sure this hammer doesn't escape." I sent another patrolman up to his car to radio for Daniels. It turned out that Daniels, after taking his photos and prints from the studio, had stopped for coffee on his way back to headquarters, so he was still in the neighborhood when he got the call. He was back at the Dawson studio in a few minutes. He carefully put the hammer into a plastic bag. Its business end was coated with blood and hair and there wasn't any doubt about its being the murder weapon. But prints would be something else.

"What do you think? Prints?" I asked him.

"Should be," he said. "High varnish handle. Want to peek a little?"

I shrugged. The lower ranks shouldn't be encouraged when they're going to violate the rules.

Daniels squatted close to the flagstone walk and,

using a cloth, carefully removed the hammer from the plastic bag. He sprinkled some white powder on it, then blew the excess off. He looked at me with a grin that my wife calls Cheshire Cat and I call shit-eating.

"See for yourself," he said. I knelt over. There were the familiar whorls, loops, and ridges of several finger-prints on the hammer grip.

"Good going," I said. "Maybe we'll have something despite ourselves."

Daniels nodded, replaced the hammer in the bag, and went back toward his car.

Leonardo was behind me, shaking his head.

"What's wrong?" I asked.

"The fingerprints."

"What about them?"

"They will be Dawson's," Leonardo said.

"Dawson? How could he . . ."

"It has nothing to do with Dawson," Leonardo said. "Someone has posed us a puzzle and is defying us to solve it."

"Yeah?"

"Yes. Our murderer. Mr. Dawson could not have thrown the hammer out here," Leonardo said. "And certainly the killer did not drop it without wiping it. And why would he just toss it gently five feet into the bushes. Why not throw it away? A hundred feet away. A thousand? It was left there for you to find."

"Why?"

"Because the killer is arrogantly insulting the po-lice."

"That's terrible. How could anyone want to insult Chief Semple? Patrolman Cantabile? Me?"

"It is wonderful," Leonardo said. "We now know that the murder is not a witless, random act, but a careful puzzle given to you by the killer. All we have to do is to solve the puzzle."

"Yeah," I said without enthusiasm. "That's all."

CHAPTER FIVE

If the Connecticut State Police had been with Columbus when he discovered America, they would have filed a report calling the trip a failure because he didn't find a route to India.

And they would have been correct.

The Connecticut State Police are always correct. Even when the whole goddam force have their heads up their asses, they're correct.

They must have all been brought up reading Winston Churchill. "Therefore comport yourselves in such a way that if the United States and its sovereign state, Connecticut, last for a thousand years, and all the crap hits all the fans in the world, the governor can still say: 'The State Police acted above reproach.'"

Thirty minutes after we found the hammer, Inspector Walter Drossner of the State Police was on the scene, being correct and acting above reproach.

I had finally gotten rid of Chief Semple. His hopes

for the immediate arrest of a crazed Numidian black-
smith having been dashed, the chief seemed willing to
go back to headquarters to prepare for his press conference. That should be a sight.

And then Drossner arrived. He is thirty-four years
old—make that eleven years younger than I am—and
while I don't dislike him for that, it helps. It also helps
that he still thinks he's going to be Hercule Poirot. I
put him in the Inspector Lestrade category myself.

Drossner showed up wearing a three-hundred-dollar
suit that would, had I worn it, have prompted an investigation by the Board of Free Selectmen. (The
Board of Free Selectmen's promulgated directive,
number 421,983,156, prohibits policemen from ex-
cessive displays of affluence, and Codicil Number 312,
Section 1, Sub-section B, paragraph F-sub One, warns
policemen against accepting any gifts of value, except
on certain specified holidays—to wit, Christmas, Father's Day, and individual birthdays, and then, only
from family and friends, and never as recompense for
normal performance of their duties.)

The suit looked correct on Drossner. Everything
did. The Ronald Colman mustache to make him look
older, the lithe athletic movements of the trim
body—I know the son-of-a-bitch rented it at the local
Jack LaLanne studio—even the small notebook he
produced from an inside jacket pocket where it did
not dare to disturb the smooth, flowing lines of his
suit.

Correct. Above reproach.

The first thing the bastard did was to cancel Chief

Semple's press conference at four o'clock, and re-
schedule one at the Dawson studio. He would handle
it himself.

He came, of course, with the usual retinue of state
police experts. This is how Connecticut works, you
know. The state police handle everything that can
possibly get a policeman's name in the papers.

"Hello, Jezail," Drossner said. Leonardo and I were
alone inside Dawson's study. "Hear you've got yourself a live one here."

"Hello, Drossner," I said.

"Got it wrapped up yet?" He let me have it, a bank
of nine hundred twelve perfect teeth, a testimonial to
the power of orthodontia. "Well, no mind, we'll have
it cleaned up soon." It was insulting that he hadn't
even waited for an answer.

He spied Leonardo sitting behind Dawson's desk
and advanced on him, his ever-extended hand jutting
out in front of him.

"How do you do, I'm Inspector Drossner, State Police."

Leonardo rose and took his hand. At an even six-
feet, he was as tall as Drossner. "Doctor Leonardo,
Misericordia College."

"Nice to meet you, Doctor. I hope you don't mind
my asking, but what are you doing here?"

I interrupted before Leonardo could answer. "I
called in the professor, Drossner. There are some unusual aspects to this case and I thought he might be
able to help. And it's all by the book. He has an appointment from the Board of Free Selectmen as a

Walton special police consultant." Which was true. I had gotten that through the board sometime the previous year, when Leonardo had helped us crack a string of vacation burglaries that had stumped us for two months, and Chief Semple had repaid him by threatening to arrest him for interfering with the police.

I could see the wheels clicking in Drossner's head and what passed for thought imprinting itself on the readout monitor behind his smooth, unwrinkled, tan forehead. *All well and good*, was what he was thinking. *If amateurs want to call in other amateurs to help them bungle along, more power to them. But professionals don't need that kind of help*. That's what he was thinking but he didn't say anything. Perhaps because he knew that, if he did, I might just punch his face out.

He contented himself with, "I trust you haven't touched anything Doctor."

"You may trust," Leonardo said.

During this conversation, Drossner's men had hovered in the doorway to the room like a bunch of dragstrip cowboys, revving up their engines, waiting for someone to drop the starting flag. I could just imagine Drossner wheeling around and shouting "go" to them, and all of them racing ahead into the room and eating the furniture.

The image made me smile. Drossner apparently didn't like smiling at a murder scene. Perhaps it was not correct and not above reproach. His voice was chilly when he said, "Suppose you fill me in, Jezail.

And we won't worry for the time being about the delay in notifying our department."

I let that pass and filled him in. I showed him where the body had been found and how. What Doctor Spears said was the cause of death and how Gunter Wilke had told us about the missing hammer and showed him where we found it. I showed him the chest of drawers that apparently had been ransacked. I told him about the prints on the hammer, on which we were awaiting word from our print man.

"The killer's prints," he said.

"Doctor Leonardo says they'll be Dawson's prints," I said.

"That doesn't make any sense."

Leonardo had been looking out the window to the left of Dawson's desk. His face was sidelit by the sinking afternoon sun. Without turning, he said, "It makes less sense for the fingerprints to belong to the killer."

"Well, I guess we'll see about that," Drossner said.

I showed Drossner the old-fashioned lock on the study door, how it could be locked only by a key and only from the inside. I showed him the key and the tie-tack that had been found in Dawson's hand.

He looked at me, his eyes narrowing almost suspiciously. "That would mean that Dawson locked the door himself," he said. "Even if there were another key, it wouldn't work outside this room. He locked the door himself."

"Seems like it."

"Then how did the weapon get outside?"

"I was expecting you to answer that," I said, hoping I didn't display as much pleasure as I felt.

Leonardo smiled at me from the window. I guess I was displaying too much pleasure.

"Before there is too much theorizing about who may have locked the door," Leonardo said, "it might be worthwhile to determine if there is another key to the door. There are ways of locking doors from the outside."

Drossner paused. "Good thought," he said. "Who would know?" he asked me.

I looked out into the unfinished part of the studio building. Old Man Wilke was still there, giving a statement to Detective Waldron.

"Mister Wilke?" I said.

He looked up.

"How many keys were there to this door?"

He held up one finger. "Those were Mr. Dawson's directions," he said, and shrugged. "So I followed them. If you do not believe me, you can ask at Solomon's lock shop. They made up one lock with one key."

"Thank you."

"Another thing," he said. "I have just remembered. Yesterday, the woman, Mrs. Dawson, came down the steps to talk to her husband. They talked. I did not hear what they said. She did not come in here."

"All right. Thanks."

I brushed by Leonardo who was coming out the door as I went back inside.

"One key," I told him and he nodded. Back inside,

I told Drossner the same thing. He nodded as if he had known it all along.

I stood by the window looking out behind the studio. Leonardo was out there, inspecting a pile of lumber, oak panels and two-by-fours, I guess, left over from the building project.

I was fishing around in my pocket for my pack of cigarettes when I found the sheet of yellow paper that I had taken from Dawson's desk to protect it from Chief Semple practicing his ABC's. I handed it to Drossner who glanced at it and said:

"What's that?"

"Just some notes from Dawson's desk," I said. "Poetry or something."

"I'm not interested in that kind of thing," he said and handed it back. I shoved it back into my pocket. "Poetry's not going to solve a murder," he said.

The telephone rang. As I picked it up, Leonardo came back in from outside. The caller was Daniels from headquarters. When I hung up, Drossner looked at me questioningly.

"The fingerprints on the hammer," I said.

"Yes?"

"Dawson's." I looked toward Leonardo. He had resumed his place at the window and was staring out toward Long Island Sound two hundred yards away, silhouetted black against the bright sunlight, the edges of his image fuzzy where the light diffused around them.

Drossner kept busy, shaking his head.

He walked over and sat behind Dawson's desk. "A

locked room mystery. Just the kind he used to write. In *Pieces of Eight . . .*" His voice trailed off. Trust him to have read Dawson. I haven't read a bestseller in fifteen years. I'm still trying to catch up with my readings from the fifties. And the older I get, the more I like to reread books I read and enjoyed before. Do we all lose our sense of adventure when we get older? Or is it that we just like to know how things will turn out?

Drossner lit a small, filter-tipped cigar that he carried in a small metal case in his vest pocket. He blew a very large smoke ring.

We were an interesting tableau. Leonardo looking out the window. Drossner blowing smoke rings. Me leaning against the chest of drawers.

Drossner blew another circle, larger than the first. He waved at his men, still hovering in the doorway, and told them to go outside and look around for clues. "Let's try to construct something, Jezail, that might fit with the known facts. Now, I'm not saying this is the way it happened. I'm just trying to find possibilities to weigh."

He blew another smoke ring. I felt like grabbing it and pulling it down over his ears.

"Dawson is hit with a hammer. A fatal blow. The murderer drops the weapon and flees. Dawson picks up the hammer, putting his prints on it. He struggles outside. He throws the hammer into the bushes. He gets back inside. He locks the door of his study. He collapses and dies with the key still in his hand. What about that? Of course, it doesn't make much sense. But we have to construct scenarios."

"That is insufficient," Leonardo said. "Even for a scenario." He still had not turned from the window. He was chewing on the end of a ballpoint pen, one of a pack he carried in his shirt.

"Why?" asked Drossner.

"Because of the blood stains. If Dawson had struggled outside to throw the hammer away, there would be some trace of blood between the study and the front door and out onto the flagstone walk. There is no blood. He moved no farther than between the door and the spot his body was found."

"Then how did the hammer get outside?" Drossner asked.

"The murderer put it there," Leonardo said.

"And why does it have Dawson's prints on it?"

"That is just another part of the puzzle," Leonardo said. "It will be solved."

"It surely will," Drossner said. "All right. Give me another scenario."

"I'm all out," I said. Leonardo continued looking out the window. If he had heard, he didn't indicate it. There was a moment's silence in the room, then Leonardo said, "The killer has laid a scenario out for you very carefully. You have just not thought of it yet."

"And you have?"

"What of the tie-tack?" Leonardo asked. He turned from the window and aimed a disarming smile at Drossner.

"What of it?" Drossner said, but he clipped the end

of the word "it." "Of course," he said. "The tie-tack."
He leaned back in the chair and blew a smoke ring in
the air, then plunged forward and slapped the desk
with his right hand. "That's it. That's it."

"What's it?" I asked.

"The scenario. And this time, it works. Dawson is
hit by the killer in a scuffle. Probably he surprised
him, burglarizing his chest of drawers there. Dawson
drops. The killer thinks he's dead. He puts the hammer into Dawson's hand to put Dawson's prints on it.
Just to confound us, maybe. Then he runs away and
throws the hammer away as he goes. But Dawson's
not dead. Dying but not dead. He knows he's dying.
He hasn't got a phone to call for help. He can't make
it to the main house. He realizes that in his hand, he's
got the killer's tie-tack, ripped off in the struggle. He
knows it will identify the killer. He wants revenge.
With his last breaths, he crawls to the door and locks
it. He starts back into the room, the key and the tie-
tack in his hand. He dies."

He blew a smoke ring, then looked up at me and
then at Leonardo.

Leonardo was smiling gently.

"Why'd he bother to lock the door?" I asked.

Drossner's lips and nose puckered up for a moment
as if he had just encountered a bad smell. He squint-
ed, thinking. His face unfurled a smile. "Naturally, he
locked the door so that the tie-tack evidence would be
conclusive. If the door was unlocked, someone could
have come in and planted evidence in his hand. Evidence to incriminate somebody else. But not with the

door locked. Don't you see, Dawson did it to give us the facts we needed to get his killer? And to make the case air-tight."

I shrugged. It annoyed me, but I couldn't find a real hole in it yet.

Drossner looked up to Leonardo. "And you, Doctor, what do you think of that scenario?"

"It is an accurate retelling of the story that was left here for us."

I caught it but Drossner didn't. I know Leonardo and the precision of his speech. He wasn't buying Drossner's explanation but Drossner didn't know that. He took what Leonardo said as affirmation.

When the press arrived for their conference fifteen minutes later, I really began to believe that Drossner had the solution. Because he spent most of his time mugging for the television cameras and telling everybody how unsolvable the crime was.

"The Locked Room Mystery," I heard him say once. And again, "The final puzzle in the life of Barry Dawson, America's master puzzler." I felt like upchucking, and not just because he managed not to mention me or Chief Semple.

He was playing the press like an accordion. He didn't mention one word about his proposed solution to the puzzle. Just how unsolvable it was. It was like the old days of the FBI. On one week, name somebody to your list of ten-most-wanted. Tell how awful, terrible, and uncatchable he is. And the next week, pick him up from where you knew he was hiding all along. Drossner was doing the same thing. Explaining how this crime could not be solved, so that when he made an arrest, one day, two days, whenever, later, he'd get the credit for solving the unsolvable crime. And if he didn't make an arrest, who could blame him? After all, the mystery was unsolvable. The bastard. He did not mention the diamond tie-tack either.

It was slick though. I think the state police go to public relations school, right after their orthodontia work is done.

Leonardo and I stood leaning against the oak-paneled wall in the Dawson living quarters, watching Drossner's routine.

Leonardo touched my arm. "Anthony, have you not yet exceeded your threshold of pain?"

I nodded. "Forty seconds after that bastard arrived."

"Let us go outside."

He turned toward the front door. I pushed away from the wall to follow him and, goddamit, ripped the left sleeve of my brand-new sports jacket on a nail sticking out of the wall. The knit fabric tore with a sound like an exhalation through pursed lips.

I shook my head at Leonardo. "Dammit," I said, "a seventy-five dollar jacket."

"A grateful public will buy you another when you solve the Dawson murder," he said softly with a smile.

Outside, he seemed content to look at the dull gray waters of Long Island Sound.

"You don't think Drossner's on the right track," I said.

"The man is an idiot."

"He sounds pretty sure of himself."

"Certainly, he is sure of himself," Leonardo said. "He is like a child's windup toy that moves single-mindedly in one direction until its batteries run out or until it marches forward into disabling disaster. He is doing exactly what the killer of Mr. Dawson wants him to do. He will continue to do just that. Fortunately, you and I are here."

"Maybe you. But me, I'm drawing nothing but blanks."

"That is why you are exceptional, Anthony. You do not know, so you do not presume. That one," he nodded over his head toward the house, meaning, of course, Drossner, "is a specialist in presumption."

"Now you know why everyone hates the Connecticut State Police," I said. We stood there silently until Patrolman Thomas Bengston came running down the stone steps from the parking area to me.

"Lieutenant, I just heard from Baker. Somebody's come back to the big house."

"Who? Did he say?"

"Yeah. Mrs. Dawson."

"Does she know about her husband?"

Bengston nodded.

I pulled him away from the house and spoke softly. "Okay. Tell Baker to stay put and make sure no reporters get in to talk to her. We'll be over as soon as Jody Powell in there finishes his bullshit story."

Bengston grinned. Nothing a patrolman likes more than to hear one superior officer put down another. It kind of confirms all his suspicions.

He nodded and went back toward the steps on a trot to rouse Baker on his car radio. And Leonardo and I just kept staring at the Sound, waiting for Drossner to finish simonizing the press corps. Leonardo didn't say much, but then he never does. He once told me, "Anthony, I find it difficult to engage my mouth without disengaging my brain. Since thought is usually more important than speech, I am often silent. You understand?"

I understood, and so I just didn't ask Leonardo questions if I could avoid it. He would answer all my questions in his own good time.

CHAPTER SIX

It took the three of us an hour to get to the main Dawson mansion. That's how long it took Drossner to finish up with the press. He marched them around Dawson's studio, giving them his song and dance, and complaining about the insoluble mystery. Insoluble. I swear to God that's the word he used. I know it's a good word, but, Christ, he's a cop, isn't he?

He was such a gracious tour guide, the son-of-a-bitch should have been wearing Mousketeer ears.

Finally he finished with the press and the three of us walked along the flagstone path away from Dawson's studio toward a flight of steps cut into the hillside. Halfway up the steps there was a small concrete landing. The way was barred by a cyclone fence with a six-foot-high gate, but it opened with one of those push bars that they have on school doors. As we passed through, Leonardo bent down and picked up what appeared to be a thin strip of yellow paper.

He paused on the landing and pointed out to me a speaker box erected next to the gate, probably connected with the speaker on Dawson's desk.

"It is unusual, is it not," Leonardo said, "that this gate locks, the gate leading to the main Dawson house? But the gate leading to the parking area on the other side of the studio has no lock on it. Would it not seem more normal if it were the other way around?"

"I guess so," I said.

Drossner was not around to hear this conversation. He was already up the steps and marching along toward the Dawson house at ninety steps to the minute, as if a talent scout for the 125th Infantry Regimental Drill Team might be lurking behind the nearest bush.

I hate soldiers and you know you've been a cop too long when you start hating soldiers on general principle. It's only a small step from there to hating cops themselves, and from that to hating your own self. Maybe by the time you start hating soldiers, it's an irreversible process. Too late to stop.

Detective Baker was in the gravel driveway when we got there and he saluted us toward the house, but I stopped to talk to him while Drossner marched on resolutely, Boris Karloff carrying his cross up the sand dune in *Lost Patrol*. Leonardo waited with me.

"Who's in there?"

"Mrs. Dawson and Dawson's assistant and some kind of handyman, I guess."

"They all come back together?"

"No. Mrs. Dawson got here first. About an hour and a half ago. The others came later. Separately."

"Okay, Baker. Stay loose. The piranhas of the press may be swarming down on you any minute. Keep them away. They'll eat the eyes out of your skull if you let them. Better yet, get a car over here and post it at the gate. Keep them out."

"Yes, sir."

We caught up with Drossner at the front door, which was just being opened by a tall man wearing overalls. Jeans imply fashionable but these were overalls. And he had on a short-sleeved cotton shirt that was red plaid and looked like it ought to be made out of flannel. He had the sloping shoulders and the long, stringy arm muscles of a man who knew what work was and knew how to do it.

"Yes?" he said.

"I'm Inspector Drossner of the State Police. This is Lieutenant Jezail of the Walton Police." He ignored Leonardo.

"Come in," the man said. He was close to sixty, I guess, but his voice sounded a hundred years old. I had the fleeting thought that perhaps we had found somebody who would mourn the passing of Barry Dawson.

While the voice sounded old, the body moved young and big and strong. The man walked briskly as he led us into the main hall of the house. I closed the door behind us and then we followed him into a sitting room off to the left. Sliding oaken doors. Luxury.

And speaking of luxury, Mrs. Barry Dawson was in the room, along with a slight man who looked like a librarian. He was wearing a tweed jacket—God strike me dead, with patches on the elbows—a button-down shirt and a tie, and brown slacks, the kind that wrinkle if you get caught in a breeze. He looked like he had spent the last fourteen days sleeping in a windstorm. With his clothes on.

Mrs. Dawson was something else again. I knew her immediately because if you read any papers at all, or "people" magazines, it would be hard to miss her picture. Fact is, I think Dawson got a lot of his publicity because magazines wanted an excuse to run Christabella Dawson's picture.

Mrs. Dawson. I should qualify that, I suppose. The fifth Mrs. Dawson. The first four had drifted off into that land of petits fours, ballet openings, world tours, and alimony.

I once read an interview in which Dawson said he had to make two hundred thousand dollars a year, just for openers—for alimony—before he started to make anything for himself. To tell you the truth, it didn't exactly choke me up feeling sorry for him.

Neither did looking at Christabella Dawson. Dawson had plucked her from a burlesque show at the Royal Casino in Las Vegas two years earlier when he was living there for awhile to get a divorce from Mrs. Dawson Number Four.

This one was about twenty-five-years-old, tall, leggy, and bosomy with the kind of gaudy sexual weaponry that always seems to wind up married to men homelier than me.

When we went into the room, she was mixing herself a drink at a portable bar situated in a bay win-

dow. She turned to look at us, then coolly went back
to finishing her drink. Johnny Walker Red on the
rocks, the rocks coming from a small automatic ice-
maker built into the bottom of the bar. Not exactly a
woman's drink, but who knows how the other half
lives.

I recognized the man in the tweed jacket. He was
Dawson's secretary, Alfred something. Needles, that
was it. Alfred Needles. I knew him because he came
to my office one day and said he was researching Connecticut police procedures for a book Dawson was
writing. This was right after the flap about Dawson
doing an exposé on Walton, and so I wound up
spending my lunch hour with Needles, trying to pump
him, and getting only a sore throat for my trouble.

He seemed like a nice enough fellow, kind of bland,
but he didn't give me any information at all, and I got
the feeling talking to him that there was more steel in
him than you might expect at first glance. He had
straight, crewcut hair and a kind of acné-battlefield
face, but his handshake had been firm, and he gave
me that feeling of toughness I sense every time I see a
professional jockey. Small but hard.

He recognized me and seemed about to say something when Drossner spoke, and Needles looked
toward him.

"Mrs. Dawson, I'm Inspector Drossner of the State
Police. This is Lieutenant Jezail of Walton."

"And this is Doctor Leonardo," I interrupted.

Mrs. Dawson nodded curtly and took a long sip of
her scotch.

"Well, let's get it over with," she said, walking over to the sofa and sitting down next to Needles. "Who killed Barry?"

"We're still investigating," Drossner said. "We thought you might be able to help us." For the first time, he seemed to notice Needles. "I'm Inspector Drossner of the State Police. Who are you?" he asked.

"I'm Alfred Needles. I'm . . . I was Mr. Dawson's secretary."

"Is there anybody else who lives in this house?" Drossner asked.

"Just Walter there," said Mrs. Dawson. She nodded to the man who had let us in. Drossner turned to him and the man said "Walter Payton." His voice sounded almost apologetic for existing. "I help out around here."

"No servants?" Drossner asked Mrs. Dawson.

"Barry didn't believe in servants. Some bullshit about the Third World not understanding. I think he was just cheap."

Drossner nodded solemnly. The man had no sense of humor at all, which tells you something about his intelligence. I have this theory that a person's intelligence can be pretty readily measured by the number and variety of different things he laughs at. The more types of humor you recognize, the smarter you are. It works all the way down to idiot level, but there the theory falls apart. Chief Semple laughs at everything.

"We might as well start with you, Mr. Needles," Drossner said. "Suppose you tell us of your where-abouts yesterday and the last time you saw Mr. Dawson."

"Oh, for Christ's sake," said Christabella. "Needles didn't kill anybody. Why are you wasting our time?"

"Well, Mrs. Dawson," Drossner said smoothly. He said everything smoothly. "Do you know who killed your husband?"

She slugged down all the scotch in her glass before shaking her head no.

"Do you know who might want to kill him? Do you have any idea of a suspect?"

"Apart from everybody who knew him, no," she said.

"Well, Mrs. Dawson, the body of your husband was found in his studio a few hours ago, his head bashed in. In his hand was found the key to the room, and it looks as if he locked the door himself before dying. It is a very complicated crime to solve and if you have no suspects for us, I really haven't any choice but to question everybody, Mrs. Dawson. I'm sure you understand."

She understood and she shut up. Drossner turned back to Needles.

"Now, about yesterday. Suppose you tell me where you were."

Needles gulped a little. His collar rose and fell and his tie lifted with it, then dropped down onto his sunken chest as if surrendering.

"I was here. All day."

"I see. And what were you doing?"

"I live here. My room is upstairs and that's where I

work, too. Mr. Dawson had me researching various kinds of poisons for a new book. I was in my room all day."

"Did anyone see you there?"

Needles hesitated. I looked over toward the main bay window. Leonardo was leaning against the sill, watching the questioning, his eyes fixed on Needles as if they were pins and Needles was a butterfly being fixed to a display board. Leonardo's eyeglasses hung from his mouth and he chewed on one of the earpieces.

"I don't think so," Needles said. "Wait. Yes. The television man came. He delivered a television set for my room."

"What time was that?" asked Drossner.

"About six o'clock, I guess."

"And after that?"

"I watched TV till about seven. Then I went into town to eat. The Golden Palace restaurant. I had a few drinks. I came back around ten, watched TV, and went to bed. I got up early today and drove into New York to use the library, and I just got back."

There was a scratching at the door, that kind of faint, insecure hope-you-don't-hear-it-so-I-can-say-you-weren't-here kind of noise that a wayward student must make on the principal's door at one of those English schools where they major in bondage and discipline.

Drossner knew his men. I had to say that for him. Because he paused in mid-question with Needles and walked back to the door and opened it. One of his men was standing in the hall, obviously frightened at

the need to interrupt the great man at work. Drossner
listened to his mumbling, then nodded. He waited by
the open door for a few moments, then stepped aside
to let this thing enter.

Thing is not altogether fair. I mean, there is no
question that it was human, and the odds were pre-
ponderantly on it being male gender. But it wore
tweed knickers, for Christ's sake, MacGregor plaid
stockings, and an ascot tie around the neck under a
paisley shirt. It was the first person I'd ever seen
dressed in what looked like Gene Sarazen's annual
contribution to the Volunteers of America.

The man had rich, pulpy lips, flared out in a Cu-
pid's-bow mouth that looked as if it spent all day, every day, sucking plate glass windows. And there were
baby blue eyes with an obvious eyelash transplant,
and blond hair that swept in beautiful long curls and
waves.

Near me, Christabella Dawson's face drooped into
actual physical loathing. "Nickie Neuter," she mumbled, half-aloud. "For Jesus's sake." She walked back
to the bar to make herself another drink.

Nickie Neuter?

Not exactly right. Its name, it told Inspector Drossner, was Alden Barkmore and it was Barry Dawson's
lawyer-cum-agent-cum-business manager and wasn't
his killing *stupid*? He had just been *shocked*, well, almost beyond *belief* when he'd heard of it.

As soon as Drossner heard Barkmore speak, he
backed away half a step as if homosexuality was con-
tagious. Barkmore apparently took that as a dismissal

because he walked away from Drossner and up toward the bar. Christabella had just finished pouring a healthy Johnny Walker Red when she realized Barkmore was standing in front of her. He was a small man and the statuesque blonde looked down at him.

"Christabella, dear, I'm really sorry," Barkmore said. He was standing so close to me now I could smell his scent. I'll be kind and say it was aftershave lotion, but, damn, it's the first aftershave I ever smelled that had an aroma as if it were made out of lilac paste and applied with a trowel.

"Oh, stop the shit, Alden," she said.

"I see you are handling your bereavement about as I would have expected. At the bar," he said. "Do you have a black mourning dress to wear? I'm sure we can sew up the cleavage so it stops short of your navel."

"You could do it," Christabella said. "You're probably pretty good with needle and thread. Do you knit?"

You know, the press really does a job on all of us. Here I am, standing here, watching this faggot and this amazon going at each other and I think of Alden Barkmore as . . . right, gay. I can't remember the last time I heard the word homosexual on television. Or read it in a newspaper. The press just breaks us down. First they try to convince us that homosexuality is just another normal sexual preference. But nobody in his right mind buys that. So they eliminate homosexual from the vocabulary and substitute gay, working on the very accurate theory that it will be easier to con-

vince people to accept *gays* than it would be to accept
homosexuals. What's in a name? Better believe it, a
whole frigging lot.

Anyway, Christabella and Alden Barkmore stood
there, almost toe-to-toe, and I was about to predict a
knockout in the first, when Drossner cleared his throat,
a big theatrical throat-clearing that sounded like he
was sending a message to Giselda in her dressing room
a half-block away to hurry up and get her tutu on because her big scene was coming up.

"We're glad you arrived, Mr. Barkmore," Drossner
said. "Perhaps you can shed some light on this tragic
incident."

"Don't ask him," Christabellá said. "He thinks it
was done by the munchkins. He thinks everything was
done by the munchkins." It suddenly dawned on me
that Christabella Dawson was rip-roaring drunk.

"Yes. Well, why don't you sit down, Mrs. Dawson.
And you, Mr. Barkmore, if you'll just have a seat.
We're trying to establish where everyone was last
night. We were just discussing this with Mr. Needles."

"I was done, Inspector," Needles said. "I ate last
night in town, I came back and went to bed, and I
went to New York early today."

Christabella walked back to the big velvet sofa
where Needles sat, a sofa that in my house would be
velveteen. She sat on the far end, away from him. As
she sat down, she clutched her scotch glass in both
hands and she burped. Barkmore sat in a chair near
me. Walter Payton who "helped out around here"
leaned against the wall on the far side of the room.

Drossner marched up and down in front of the assemblage.

"When was the last time you saw Mr. Dawson alive?" he asked, turning quickly toward Needles and leaning over, very close to him.

I felt Leonardo turn behind me, away from the window, to watch the questioning.

"Let's see," Needles said. "It wasn't yesterday. I didn't see him yesterday. The day before yesterday. He came up to my room where I work. He told me he wanted research on poisons. He wanted to know if there'd been any new poisons discovered in recent years that would kill people slowly but leave no trace in autopsies."

Drossner nodded. "Are there any?"

"Yes. I found quite a few of them in the New York library. There's . . ."

"Oh, come on," Christabella said thickly. "Barry wasn't poisoned. He had his head beat in. What the hell are we worrying about poisons for?"

"If I were you, I'd always worry about poisons," Barkmore answered.

Christabella hiccupped. She was out of it now. Some women—and some men—get drunk like that. One moment fine, the next moment blotto.

I guess Drossner decided to question her before she passed out.

"All right. When did you last see your husband, Mrs. Dawson?"

Christabella took a long, healthy sip of her scotch.

"Yesterday afternoon."

"About what time was that?"

"I don't know. Four o'clock maybe."

"Did you see him here? In the house?"

"No. I went down to the studio. He had that god-dam gate locked. He always has the gate locked. But I buzzed him on the intercom. He's got a speaker setup there. I wanted to talk to him. But he couldn't hear me. Those goddam workmen were making so much noise, hammers flying and electric saws screeching, that he couldn't hear me, and I finally yelled for him to come up to the fence 'cause I couldn't get in 'cause the goddam gate was locked. Can you imagine that, his wife, and I couldn't even go to his office?" She looked at Drossner, hoping to find some sympathy there for the outrage she had suffered. His face was as blank as it always was.

"Anyway," she said, "he finally came out and he was nasty to me as usual."

"What was he nasty about?" asked Drossner.

She shrugged. "Barry didn't need a reason to be nasty."

I watched faces. Alfred Needles didn't agree with this and neither did Walter Payton, whose face got red and angry. I couldn't see Barkmore's face but he was shaking his head slightly.

"Oh, I remember. I told him I needed some money to go shopping. He told me to get a job. That's the way he talked to me, his wife. I told him what he could do and he slapped me. Right in the face."

"What did you do then?"

"I called him a name and I went away. And I drove

into New York for dinner and I stayed over and I didn't come back last night."

Drossner nodded. He was one of those cops who has trouble thinking of the next question to ask. I could see he was struggling.

"What did you call him?" he finally asked, after a long pause.

"You want to know?"

"Yes, ma'am."

"I called him a rat bastard prick cocksucker," Christabella said. "Wait a minute." She sipped her drink again. "Maybe it was a prick bastard rat cocksucker. I'm not sure. No, no. It was rat bastard prick cocksucker. I'm sure of it now. That's what I always called him."

Drossner seemed embarrassed to have gotten involved. "And that was the last time you saw him? Or spoke to him?"

She had her glass to her mouth again and couldn't talk so she nodded, and spilled some of the scotch on her maroon dressing gown.

"It does seem strange," Drossner said, "that the gate was kept locked."

"Mr. Dawson liked privacy for his work, sir," said Walter Payton, in a voice that sounded as if it came from beyond the grave.

When Drossner looked at him, he said "Dawson did not like interruptions, Mr. Drossner."

"How could he work then, with a new kitchen being put in?" Drossner asked.

"That was different, sir," Payton said. "Mr. Dawson

used to be a newspaperman and he was prideful
that he could work anywhere, with any kind of noise.
But he could not work with conversation, where
people were liable to interrupt him by talking to him.
That's why he couldn't work around the house and
why I installed the speaker system last month. He
didn't like being bothered. But he was a fine man. A
fine man." His voice trailed off as if he were remem-
bering only the good times.

"He was a rat bastard prick cocksucker," Christabella contributed thickly. I saw Walter clench his big
knotty fists. Now if I had seen that and if Christabella
had been the corpse, I would have had a pretty good
idea of one suspect for my list. Payton was protective
of Barry Dawson even after death. Who knows? Everybody has somebody who likes him.

"Do you know I was never in that studio? He
wouldn't let me through the gate? You know that?"
Christabella said. "You, Needles. You ever get in
there?" She pointed a finger at Needles. Unfortunately, the finger was attached to the scotch glass and
she spilled some of the whisky on the couch. "Whoops,"
she said. "You ever in the studio, Needles?"

Needles shook his head.

"See. What I tell you?" she demanded of Drossner.
"He didn't like nobody. Rat bastard prick cocksucker." She had it down right now and she spilled out
the seven syllables as if they were one word that she
had spent a week learning to pronounce smoothly.

Drossner tried to ignore her. "When did you last
see Mr. Dawson, Walter?"

"Yesterday morning, sir," Payton said. His voice was thick, deep, and sorrowful. "I made breakfast for the two of us, sir, in the kitchen, as I always did. And when we were done eating, he said to me, 'Wally,' he said, 'why don't you go see your mother today?' He knew I'd been wanting to see her for a long time. So he told me to go. It was like him, to be thoughtful like that."

"Ha," said Christabella.

"Where does your mother live?" Drossner asked.

Payton recoiled just a fraction. If people spoke in a regular rhythm, his answer was off by one beat. "She's ill, Inspector. She's in a hospital."

"Where?"

"Up north. She's in Syracuse."

"So you went up there?"

"Yes. I did the breakfast dishes and then I drove up. But I had car trouble last night. I called the house to say I wouldn't be back until today, but nobody answered."

"When did you call the house?" asked Drossner.

"About eight o'clock, eight-thirty."

Drossner nodded. "Were *you* ever in Mr. Dawson's studio?"

"Yes, sir, like I said, a couple of weeks ago I put in the speaker system to the gate."

"And since then?"

Payton shook his head. "Mr. Dawson liked his privacy."

"I see."

"He was a frigging loony," Christabella said. "All

loonies like to be alone. To communicate with the great loony in the sky. Maybe get in a few words with the munchkins. That right, Barkmore? That how you loonies do it?"

Barkmore whirled in his seat, about to respond in kind, but Drossner interrupted. "You, Mr. Barkmore. What was it that brought you here?"

Barkmore hesitated as if he'd rather peel Christabella's skin than answer Drossner, but he finally sank back into his chair and turned to Drossner, carefully crossing his knicker-clad legs. Knickers, for God's sakes.

"I just got back today from the coast," he said. "I was putting together a movie deal for *Pieces of Eight*, Barry's last book. Pacino, Nicholson, Hoffman, and Redford are interested. When I got to my office there was a note from Barry that I should come up and talk to him right away. Important. So I came *right* up. And then when I was driving, I heard the news and nearly drove right off the road, I was so shocked. Between the jet lag and the horror, well, I *nearly* went into a ditch."

"You should have," said Christabella.

"That's enough out of you, Pussy Galore," snarled Barkmore.

"Mr. Barkmore, please," said Drossner. "You said you were to talk to Mr. Dawson about business. What kind of business? Can you tell me that?"

"Gladly. I think Barry wanted to take this bitch out of his will."

Christabella was protecting her scotch now with

both hands. "Let 'im," she said. "I'll have it over-
turned as the work of a loony and his munchkin."

"Is that what Mr. Dawson said in the message you
got?" asked Drossner.

"Not exactly. He just said business. But he's often
mentioned changes in his will. In the past, he has
talked to me about dropping Queen Isabella from his
list of beneficiaries." He turned toward her and smiled
sweetly. "I guess, under the assumption that she could
always make a living. Anywhere there is a street to
walk."

"Do you have the note from Mr. Dawson?" asked
Drossner.

"It's back in my office," said Barkmore. "I will get
it to you if you feel it's important."

"Yes. I do. Very important," Drossner said. He
threw me a look that was all sweet triumph. It gave
me a strange feeling; I hadn't realized we were on opposite sides.

"Actually, Barry's will is very simple," Barkmore
said.

Drossner raised his hand and cut him off. "Yes, yes.
We'll get to that later."

I didn't know what he was up to, whether he might
have been trying to prevent Christabella from getting
nervous at knowing that he knew what was in
Dawson's will. If that's what it was all about, he could
have saved the effort, because Christabella was asleep,
still clutching her glass with both hands. Two of the
frittered-away ice cubes were melting neatly on her
lap. It raised a difficult question in etiquette. Do you

walk over and remove the ice cubes from her lap and run the risk of her waking up and deciding you were trying to molest her? Or do you just let them melt and give her a cold, wet box?

Leonardo stepped past me to Christabella and plucked the ice cubes gently from her lap and dropped them into a wastepaper basket near the bar. She smiled in her sleep. His faint touch must have brought back pleasant memories.

There was another scratching at the door that could only indicate one of Drossner's state police cat people.

Drossner talked to the man in the doorway for a moment.

"Folks," he said when he turned back. "The press is outside and clamoring about deadlines. So I'm going to go talk to them. Perhaps, Mr. Barkmore, you'd come out and say a few words on behalf of the family."

"Certainly," Barkmore said. "I can tell them that Christabella is sedated. The way I know that is that she is not in rut."

"Munchkin," she mumbled.

"And then my men and I will talk to each of you individually and take statements covering the ground we just went over." Drossner looked around as if waiting for questions. There were none.

"Lieutenant Jezail, you want to go out with me and talk to the gentlemen of the fourth estate?"

"No. You go ahead, Inspector Drossner," I said.

He nodded as if that were the correct way for things to be done.

CHAPTER SEVEN

I joined Leonardo at the bay window that looked
out over the rolling green lawns of the Dawson estate.
At the far edge of the main lawn was a stand of pine
trees, bordering the drop into the gully where Barry
Dawson's studio was located.

"I want to see this man's room, this Needles,"
Leonardo said.

"No problem. Why?"

"Because I believe he is going to be arrested for this
killing." Leonardo's voice was a soft whisper, and as
he spoke, he twisted around in his fingers the yellow
paper strip he had picked up before near the gate
leading down to the studio.

"Any reason why he should be arrested?" I said, as
I turned to watch the people in the room.

"The tie-tack." He said it as if those words explained everything. Maybe they did to him, but they

didn't do a thing for me. I waited but he did not volunteer anything else.

"What about the tie-tack?" I said.

Leonardo looked toward me as if he were a teacher and I were a pupil asking him a question he had answered just moments before. It seemed as if I weren't there and only the stupidity of my question existed, hanging in the air. It's why I hate to ask him questions. Then his face softened. He replaced the piece of yellow paper in his pocket.

"If you look at Mr. Needles's tie, you will see there is a hole in the precise center of the fabric where the fibers have been broken by a tie-tack. The hole is quite large. He wears a tie-tack regularly. He is not wearing a tie-tack today. Even Inspector Drossner will notice that."

I looked around casually. Needles was sitting on the couch. Drossner was standing in front of him, leaning forward slightly from the waist, as if he'd learned it in a book on getting and keeping executive power. He was waiting for Barkmore to go outside with him to the press. Barkmore was adjusting his cravat.

"I couldn't see any hole in Needles's tie and told Leonardo that.

"You are too far away," he said.

"You're even farther away than me."

"But I see differently," he said. "And now I want to see his room."

"All right. We'll get up to his room. Any special reason?"

"Yes. I want to see how his television set works." His voice trailed off as his attention drifted away from me, almost a physical process, his intellect floating away from my reach, traveling somewhere to a different dimension.

Drossner and Barkmore left the room to go outside and lie to the reporters. Needles got up from the couch and I went over to join him. He was looking at Christabella with a look that was perhaps just sympathy, perhaps something else. She snored noisily on. Needles seemed confused and he glanced toward Walter Payton who nodded, then came over and in his strong arms lifted Christabella off the couch as if she were a sleeping baby.

"I'll take her upstairs, Alfred," he said.

"Thank you. The strain obviously has gotten to her more than she would like to show."

Payton slid open a side door of the room and carried Christabella out with no more effort than that needed to carry a two-dollar handful of groceries.

Needles said to me, "I remember you. We met at your office some time ago."

"Yeah, I remember." He seemed relieved as if he were not used to being remembered. "And this is Doctor Leonardo."

I looked toward the window but Leonardo had gone.

"He went out with Wally," Needles said. "But I've heard of him. So had Barry." Speaking Dawson's name seemed to fill him again with the realization that his employer was dead.

"What do you think happened?" I asked him.

"I don't know. I just don't know. I know Barry had this image as a loudmouth and a trouble-maker, but he was really a kind and decent man. Everybody liked him."

"It doesn't sound much like Christabella was likely to confuse him with Saint Francis of Assisi."

"They were having their troubles. That's why he put up that gate and that speaker system. That's why he started working in the studio building before it was even done. When he was trying to work around here, Christabella would just harass him all the time. He had to get away from her. I can't really blame him, could you?"

"Some men live too well and marry too badly," I said. And here I've been complaining about Drossner saying stupid things. I do it a lot when I can't think of anything else to say, and then after I say something stupid, I wish I had just been quiet.

He nodded, and I said, "Do you mind if we go upstairs to your room?"

"No. Of course not. Will it be all right with Inspector what's-his-name?"

"No problem," I said.

Needles's room was in a corridor at the top of the main staircase. The front door was open behind us as we walked up, and I heard Barkmore's mincy voice coming from outside:

"It was a terrible shock to all of us. Barry Dawson was one of the finest men I have ever known. Mrs. Dawson will be unable to see anyone for awhile. She has been sedated and is resting. The strain of the day has just been too much for her."

I could almost picture the nasty little smirk on his face as he was talking to the press. Then Drossner's voice cut into Barkmore's and I blocked them out.

My face must have registered something because Needles said to me, "Alden's really a very brilliant man. He handled all Barry's business matters and Barry trusted him without question."

As we went into Needles's room, Walter Payton came out of a room farther down the hall at the end of the hallway, probably the master bedroom. He nodded to Needles.

"Thank you, Wally," Needles said.

Needles's room was bigger than some apartments I've lived in and busier than some libraries.

It was like a two-room apartment without a wall separating the rooms. At the far end, there was a large brass bed and dressers and wall-to-wall closets. A brown suit and a white shirt were draped over the back of a chair near the bed.

At the end we came in, the room was filled, floor to ceiling, with wall-to-wall bookshelves, the kind I always try to build but that always winds up tilted or crooked or loose at one end. Some books. The shelves were meticulously labelled "poison," "weapons," "mutilation." Ghastly, but all very neat. Needles was a man who knew something about death. There was also a couch, and a huge wooden desk with a typewriter stand built into one of the sides. There were two sheets of paper in the typewriter. Trust Needles not to type without using a backup sheet of paper. He seemed the type.

I bet he also cleaned his roller with carbon tetrachloride after every 10,000 words. I know you're supposed to do that because the Board of Free Selectmen told us all in a missive entitled: *Typewriters, Proper Care Of*.

Across from the couch was a television set on a stand, one of those nice Japanese portable color jobbies that I keep looking at and expecting to buy someday if I can ever find a way to make my Sears Silvertone break down. Which grows increasingly doubtful. The color is now so washed out that it makes Toulouse Lautrec's palette look absolutely garish, but the damned set just won't die.

The television set was on and Leonardo was standing in front of it, looking at it. The picture was awful looking, kind of washed with blue.

"I was waiting for you," Leonardo said to Needles, as if that explained his presence in the room. "Did you watch television today, Mr. Needles?" he asked.

"No. I went right to New York."

"So you only watched television last night after the set was delivered?"

"That's right."

"Do you like the color this way?" Leonardo asked.

"I don't know." Needles looked at the set as if seeing it for the first time. "It's all right, I guess. I adjusted it last night. Maybe it's a little blue. I guess it is."

"Yes, it is," Leonardo agreed. He turned to Needles

with a smile on his handsome face. When Leonardo chose to be charming, he could take off your socks without unlacing your shoes.

Needles ran a hand over his face, as if to wipe away exhaustion and fatigue, and then slumped into the couch. Leonardo stepped over and put his hand on the man's shoulder. "It's all right," he said.

Dawson's assistant looked up, as if Leonardo had been able to see through his skull and read what was written on his mind. He searched Leonardo's face as if looking for some kind of hope there. Leonardo again patted the man's shoulder.

"I don't know," Needles said. "I just get the feeling that . . . well, that Inspector Drossner . . . I . . ."

"Do not worry, Mr. Needles," Leonardo said. "Whatever may happen, Lieutenant Jezail and I will be here. We will see that justice is done."

Walking down the stairs, I asked Leonardo, "What was that all about? I keep getting the feeling that I missed something, like I walked in in the middle of the movie."

"It is very simple, Anthony. Mr. Needles is afraid, and with cause, that he is going to be charged with the Dawson murder. You and I know he did not do it."

"We do?"

"And I merely wanted to let him know that we are on his side and will stand with him."

"Of course we will," I said. "I just wish I knew why."

Leonardo shrugged. "Because his television set is

too blue, and there was nothing in his trouser cuffs."

When we reached the hallway downstairs, Drossner was just coming back inside with Alden Barkmore. The agent looked smugly satisfied, as if he had just done a good day's work. He flitted around like a nervous hummingbird until Drossner dismissed him.

"Mr. Barkmore, would you please wait for me and my men in the study? Then we'll start taking everyone's statements. I have to speak to Lieutenant Jezail for a moment."

Barkmore nodded and went into the large front room. When the door closed behind him, Drossner looked for a moment at Leonardo as if his presence would make it impossible for him to talk. Then he talked anyway.

"I want to keep an eye on these people for a day or so," he said.

"And then you will make your arrest," Leonardo said. It was not a question but a statement of fact.

Drossner seemed surprised. "Perhaps," he said cautiously.

"The tie-tack, of course," said Leonardo.

"Of course," Drossner said, reluctantly. He was amazed that Leonardo knew. I was never amazed at anything Leonardo knew. "Good guess," he grudgingly admitted.

"Guessing is for those who do not know," said Leonardo.

"All right. How did you *know*?"

"You did not mention the tie-tack when you were

questioning those people inside. It would have been highly ordinary to mention it. You therefore had a reason not to, since your questioning was highly ordinary. What other reason than your plan to save it to confront your suspect later, under a more controlled atmosphere, when there is more chance of his breaking down? The tie-tack is his, by the way."

"Where is he?"

"He is up in his room," Leonardo said. This conversation that had started between Drossner and me now excluded me.

"I take it you disagree with my suspicion," said Drossner.

"It is not for me to agree or disagree with your conclusion, at least not until I can prove it incorrect."

"But your feeling?" asked Drossner.

"My feeling is that you are doing exactly what the murderer wanted you to do."

"We'll see about that," Drossner said.

"Yes, we will," Leonardo said.

Drossner told me he would drop off copies of the statements his men took at Walton police headquarters and he would make no arrest before calling me in first. This is standard operating procedure to make sure there are no jurisdictional arguments in court about the state police's right to arrest.

I nodded, and Drossner walked to the front door, snapped his fingers, and his crew scurried in. I mean scurried. They followed him into the front room where Barkmore was waiting.

"The man is a dermoid cyst," Leonardo said.

"A what?"

"A dermoid cyst. It has hair and fingernails. But no brains."

Seemed about right to me.

As we turned to leave, I heard a faint sound in the side hallway behind us. Before I could look to see what it was, Leonardo had moved to the hallway and was looking down it.

"Goodbye, Walter," he said. "We will see you again."

He paused a moment, then followed me outside.

"Mr. Payton was smiling," he said.

My car was still parked on the far side of Dawson's studio, so we took the short cut, down the steps past the scene of the murder.

As we walked across the grass, the late afternoon sun threw our shadows out long and deep in front of us.

The locked gate had been tied open now with a rope, and there was a sign on a rope hanging across the opening.

POLICE LINE
DO NOT CROSS.
STATE POLICE

Leonardo stopped to examine the gate. He seemed to be checking to see how close the mesh of the gate came to the mesh of the fence when the gate was fully opened. Finally he seemed satisfied and followed me.

"If Drossner's going to arrest Needles, why doesn't he do it right away? Tonight?"

"There are several reasons, Anthony. First he has

to confront him with the evidence of the tie-tack and make sure that it is his."

"You said it was. How do you know that?"

"When I went to Mr. Needles's room, I examined it carefully. He owns only three ties. They are all punctured the same way from a tie tack, so he wears one regularly. But there was no tack in any of his ties. And there was none on his dresser or in his jewelry box where he keeps two pairs of cufflinks, a broken wrist watch, and studs for a tuxedo shirt. But there was no tie-tack. Add to that the fact that the tie-tack found in Barry Dawson's hand was engraved with a pen, and that Mr. Needles is in the writing business, and I think it is rather evident the tie-tack is his."

"You said there were several reasons why Drossner didn't arrest Needles right away."

We were walking now along the flagstone path that led to the Dawson studio and Leonardo peered in the broken window. Dawson's writing room was already in semidarkness.

"Really, Anthony," said Leonardo. "You know Inspector Drossner. He has spent the better part of this day convincing the press that this is the greatest murder puzzle of all time. You know that he will wait to give those stories time to appear before arresting poor Mister Needles. What is the point in solving an 'insoluble' crime unless you first have let everyone know that it is 'insoluble'?"

"My friend, Leonardo. The public relations expert."

He laughed. "Unfortunately for your Inspector

Drossner, it will not all be as simple as he wishes. Particularly when you and I prove Mr. Needles innocent."

"And how will we do that?"

"By proving someone else guilty. Is there any other way?"

CHAPTER EIGHT

The autopsy report from Doc Spears arrived soon
after five o'clock and it came directly to me because
Chief Semple had gone home to watch himself on television.

Now if I were Chief Semple, I think the last thing I
would want to do would be to watch myself on television. Scratch that. If I were Chief Semple, the first
thing I would do would be to take my own life, which
kind of renders the whole point academic.

It made me feel warm all over to think of the chief
and Mother Semple and all the simple little Semples
eating popcorn, sitting in front of the television, and
trying to understand all the big words they used.

I had driven Leonardo back to Misericordia so he
could get his automobile and then I returned to my office.

The autopsy report from Spears and the state medical examiner was very precise. Death was caused by a

massive skull fracture, the result of a blow or blows with a hammer. The blows were delivered with extreme force. Bits of hair that matched Barry Dawson's were found on the hammer. The blood type of the stains on the hammer matched Dawson's.

The time of death was sometime between four p.m. and seven p.m. the previous day, which fit in with what Christabella said about arguing with Dawson at around four o'clock.

At 5:17 p.m., Detective Jim Glennon came into my office.

"What a freaking waste," he said.

"What is the republic doing today to offend you?"

"We've got a murder. Christ knows it's the first freaking murder in this freaking town since we slaughtered a freaking Indian tribe. And where am I? At a school talking to a pack of freaking juvenile delinquents. Career day, my ass."

"Just think. In the year two-thousand-and-one when we have another murder, maybe it'll be solved by one of the people who came into police work because they were thrilled by the example you set today."

"Shit on that. I want in. Who do you want me to book?"

"We have to wait for Inspector Drossner," I said. "He's in charge of the investigation."

"Balls. They get all the good stuff."

"But it's all right this time," I said. "He's going to fall right on his face. Book the wrong guy."

"Yeah?" said Glennon, his suspicious face pinched up even more by distrust. "How do you know that?"

"Because the television set was too blue."

"Huh?"

"And there was nothing in his cuffs."

"Huh?"

"Never mind. You had to be there."

"I'm going home," he said, convinced that his peerless leader's ripcord didn't open anymore. When he sat around that night at the Ship's Light Saloon, swapping lies with the other cops, he'd be able to tell them how Jezail finally flipped under the strain. And maybe with a new commander of detectives, they'd be able to get themselves some Magnums. Oh, well, an expectable reaction. And like most things cops did, up front and open. I don't think I could ever stand to be a boss of some firemen. I've never met a sane fireman. They have so much time to kill, lying on their bunks, staring at the ceiling, eating cold spaghetti, waiting for bells to ring, that they hatch all these insane paranoid plots. I really think all the Kennedy assassination conspiracy nonsense started in a firehouse someplace. Listening to firemen talk is like visiting the outpatient clinic at your local funny farm. It has to be seen and heard and it's still not believable.

Anyway, Detective Glennon was interruption number one.

Interruption number two was our First Selectman. That's the equivalent of mayor in a sane community.

An old maid in a paisley dress carrying a parasol. First Selectman Milton. Except she doesn't like the title First Selectman. What I really think she'd settle for is Empress or Czarina but failing that she likes to

be called First Selectperson. Another liberal twit. I
hope she gets married someday and has a son who
grows up to be a second-base-person for the L.A.
Dodgers. Or the Mets. That'd serve her right.

She was on the phone.

"Yes, Miss Milton."

"About this letter on the Magnums."

"Yes, ma'am."

"I just want you to know that I'll present it to the
Board of Free Selectmen but I doubt that they'll ap-
prove it."

"Thank you. I appreciate your effort and what's
more, the men will, too."

She was a pain in the ass but not too dumb to politic when she could.

Then she got down to the reason for the call.

"Busy day today, I guess."

"Yes, ma'am."

"The Barry Dawson case. I saw the early bulletins
on television."

"Very puzzling case indeed," I agreed.

"It would be nice to dispose of it as rapidly as possible," she said.

"I feel that way, too. Inspector Drossner of the
State Police has come to take charge."

"I see," she said. "Why don't you invite that nice
Professor Leonardo. See if he can help."

"I certainly will, ma'am. It's just the kind of thing
he's good at." Score one for our side. Leonardo's in-
volvement was now official.

"You know, Lieutenant, you hear all kinds of

rumors about a thing like this. Was Mr. Dawson's body . . . well, you know, mutilated?"

"Mutilated how, Miss Milton?"

"Well, we heard . . . there was a rumor . . . you know, some kind of sexual attack, on him. Anything to that?"

I could just picture the old dip sitting in her house, talking on the telephone, rearranging her dusty doilies, hoping to hear the filthy sexual details of the Dawson murder.

"No, ma'am. Nothing to that. His head was bludgeoned in with a claw hammer. Brains on the carpet, blood all over, bits of bone on his clothes, that kind of thing. But mutilation? I should hope not."

"Thank you, Lieutenant Jezail." Very frosty tone. No goodbye. Just a click of the phone in my ear. Maybe her vibrator battery died.

I don't think I'm ever going to be chief of this department.

Interruption three was one of Drossner's aphids, who came skulking into my office with carbons of the statements taken from the people at the Dawson house.

Alfred Needles. Walter Payton. Alden Barkmore. None from Christabella Dawson. It must have been hard to transcribe a snore.

"The inspector says be sure to read the one from Needles," the man said. "And keep it to yourself." He talked fast as if he wanted to get it all out before he was discovered.

"Thanks," I whispered, and looked around as if searching my office for spies. "Got it."

He looked at me as if the two of us, alone in the world, shared a life-and-death secret. Then he left.

I read the statement from Needles and the other statements, then I bundled them up, stuck them in my pocket and decided to drive to Leonardo's.

Walton is and has been a class town. When it was discovered in the twenties by rich New Yorkers, there were more buyers for property than there were properties to sell, so houses took on a value that had nothing to do with their size or their construction. Even houses we would call small today wound up with a carriage house or a servant's bungalow on the grounds. Welfare and the minimum wage and inflation have changed all that. There are no more carriages in the carriage houses and no servants in the servants' bungalows. Instead they're rented out for upwards of $350 a month—make your own heat—and there is no shortage of takers.

Leonardo lived in a converted carriage house, just inside a stone wall and next to the driveway that led to "the master's house," on Burying Beach Road.

At the end of the road is Burying Beach, which got its name from a Revolutionary War battle fought there between the Colonials and the British trying to land their boats. I'm told they fought for six days without casualties, and the British finally left because the boredom was too much for them. One of the Colonists died of gout. He was buried nearby and ever after it was known as Burying Beach.

For the last twenty years that I know of, Walton's been trying to get the federal government to declare the place a national historical shrine, to commemorate the brave Americans who gave their lives there in the battle for freedom. The feds, wisely, always ignore the suggestion. I mean, if you go to Burying Beach National Shrine, before long you'll have the Jersey City Apple-Jack Drinking Memorial Park and the Rhinebeck Rout Shrine and who knows what else. Bunker Hill's enough for me.

Leonardo's white Cord was in the driveway next to his house. The building itself was a three large rooms and a massive stone fireplace that ran the whole length of one wall.

The house was like Leonardo's mind. It was filled but there was order to it. Every square inch of wall space was shelved and seemed to be filled with books, with magazines in twelve-copy binders, and with manuscripts. There were models of devices, elaborate things that I could not understand, but of which the models had to be at least as impressive as whatever the real objects themselves were supposed to be. Some walls were filled with paintings done by Leonardo, most of them of horses. And they were good. Better than good.

The place looked like the best of the Smithsonian Institute, packed into three rooms.

There was one painting in particular that always knocked me out. It was a painting of a mouth. Three-feet long, two-feet high. Just a mouth. It hung over a narrow table. There were paints on the table and Leonardo always seemed to be dabbing at the mouth with a brush. Which is just what he was doing when I entered.

"That mouth again. Aren't you ever going to finish it?"

He put down the brush he held in his left hand.

"Not until I get it done correctly. I have always had trouble with mouths."

"It looks fine to me."

"Perhaps. But it does not look like the model's mouth."

"Who's the model? Anyone I know?"

He looked at me with a small warm smile. He had changed clothes and was wearing a short-sleeved sweatshirt and black chinos. He wore Adidas sneakers without socks. His eyeglasses were propped up on top of his head.

"That is most unlikely," he said. "Most unlikely."

It didn't seem so unlikely to me. The mouth seemed sort of familiar. As if I'd seen it before on someone. But . . . who knows? One of his girl friends probably. I hadn't come to see him to inspect his paintings.

"I've got the statements that Drossner took up at the Dawson house. The tie-tack belongs to Needles."

"Yes, it does. Would you like some wine?"

"What are you pushing?"

"Any variety as long as it is cheap red wine," he said.

"Fine. Just don't mix it with water."

"It is your stomach," he said.

He poured the wine from a large jug of cheap Chianti he kept in the refrigerator.

"What did Mr. Needles say?" he asked.

"I brought you the statement. Drossner finessed him. He started questioning him by complimenting him on his tie. Then he 'suddenly noticed' the small hole in the center and he got Needles talking about the tie-tack that Barry Dawson gave him a few years ago. A pen on it, and a diamond in it. He said he wasn't wearing it because he lost the clip that holds it on a couple of weeks ago. So he stuck it in his jewelry box and it's still there. That's what he told Drossner."

"Drossner did not mention that the tie-tack was found in Dawson's hand?" asked Leonardo.

"No."

"So of course Mr. Needles will have no idea how the tie-tack came to be in Dawson's studio," Leonardo said. He brought back the glasses, mine a deep red, his a pale pink mixture of wine and water.

"Red wine with water will keep you alive," he said. "Red wine without water will make you wish you were dead."

"If I had to drink red wine with water," I said, "I'd just as soon *be* dead."

I had plopped into a soft glove leather couch, facing the fireplace, unused on this warm April night. Over the mantle was a hand-painted sign on wood, painted in a white enamel with italic letters:

Impatience is the mother of stupidity.

Knowledge is the mother of love.

Science is the knowledge of things possible.

I took the glass and nodded toward the sign. "Who said that?" I asked.

"I did. One of my students made the sign."

He leaned against the fireplace wall and sipped at his watered wine. I know the old Romans did it, but I never saw anybody else do it in my life. I tried it once and it was ghastly.

"So tomorrow afternoon, Inspector Drossner will arrest Mister Needles."

"You seem pretty sure of that."

"What else can he do, considering who and what he is? The tie-tack is a strong piece of evidence. And there is something in Mr. Needles' past, something of which he is frightened, that makes him even more of a suspect. No, the inspector will arrest him in the afternoon tomorrow."

I was amused by his sureness.

"Afternoon?" I said. "Care to pick a time?"

"After twelve-fifteen," he said.

"Why after twelve-fifteen?"

"Because that is the final press time for Saturday's afternoon newspapers. The inspector would not wish to have the story of how he has singlehandedly solved the crime of the century buried in a Saturday paper. So he will wait and he will let all Saturday's papers carry the complicated murder story and then he will announce Mr. Needles's arrest in time for full coverage in the Sunday papers."

He turned around to look at the sign over the fireplace. "Indeed, impatience is the mother of stupidity. Imagine, Anthony, millions of people across this country sitting at home on Sunday, their feet up on cocktail tables, coffee cups in hand, reading about Inspector Drossner's swift and telling genius."

He spun around and the look on his face was absolutely gleeful.

"And of course he is wrong and you and I must be sure that the press manages to treat his stupidity just as fully and thoroughly as they treat his self-proclaimed genius."

"We could do it better if we could solve the frigging crime," I said.

"How little trust you have," Leonardo said.

"I trust you."

"Trust yourself. A puzzle has been posed for us, but the mind of man is the key that unlocks all puzzles. We will solve this one, too."

"Well, you'd better. You are officially on this case at the direction of the First Selectman."

"Selectperson, I believe she calls herself."

"She can call herself anything she wants. She suggested that I ask that nice Professor Leonardo to help clear up this case."

"And so, Anthony, again you see the wisdom of petting dogs and stroking homely old maids. Someday, if you follow my example, you may yet walk in the footsteps of your illustrious Chief Semple. Are those the statements?" He pointed to the pile of papers in the side pocket of my once-beautiful and now rippedy-sleeved seventy-five-dollar sports jacket.

"Yeah. I made copies for you."

He took the papers and leaned back against the fireplace to read them.

As he did I wandered around his living room. There were three books on the table underneath the painting of the mouth. Damn, that mouth was familiar. A woman's mouth, a faint, half-hearted smile, and I wish I could have placed just whose mouth it was.

The three books were by Barry Dawson. They were *Pieces of Eight*, his last book, which Drossner said he had read. And there was *Slice of Life* and *Wages of Sin*. I hadn't read any of them. I opened up *Pieces of Eight* but I only got to the inscription: "For a lousy burglar and a great friend" when Leonardo cleared his throat.

"There is nothing in these reports that we did not expect to find," he said.

I had read an eight-word inscription and he had read eleven pages of typewritten reports.

"And there are things," he said, sipping from his wine again, "that I had hoped to find but did not."

"Sins of omission," I said.

"Omission is not always just a sin. Sometimes it is a calculated act. Where did Christabella Dawson spend last night? I would like to know that, and it is amazing that Drossner's men did not ask that question. Also, Alden Barkmore came here to discuss changing Barry Dawson's will. His statement says he does not know what changes were contemplated but I would like to know what Mr. Dawson's will now awards to different parties."

He was about to say something more when there

was a knock on the door. A delivery boy had a package for Leonardo.

"My boss said he could only get seven of the books you wanted."

"That will do nicely," Leonardo said. "Be sure to thank him for me." He tipped the teenager a dollar, closed the door, and put the package on the coffee table at my feet.

"These are more of Dawson's books," he said and let out a slight sigh. "Martin Luther was right. Once in a while, we should let God run the world and just go fishing. Unfortunately, this is not one of those days."

"I'll get out of your hair. Maybe I'll even go home and see if my wife is still living with me."

"And how is Adele?" He was already opening the package of books and his mind was leaving me.

"She's fine. Mean, venial, hateful, bitter, jealous, and self-destructive. She's normal."

"She is woman. Do not expect cows to whistle," Leonardo said without looking up. He had the first Dawson book out of the package. *Tools of the Trade.*

"Dawson's first book," he said. "Published in 1959."

When I left, he said nothing. I don't think he even noticed I was gone. He was kneeling on the floor in front of the coffee table, apparently arranging the books in order of publication date.

Adele was waiting for me at home in the small Cape Cod house we own that's too close to the town's main beach to avoid the summer traffic and too far away from the water to be able to get beach-view prices for the property.

I say she was waiting, but only in the sense that a spider in his web waits for one particular fly.

Supper wasn't waiting. Warm words of welcome home after a tough day weren't waiting.

What was waiting was Adele, lying on the couch, ever-present martini in hand, watching television. When I came in, she looked up. No hello. We're beyond the stage of hello.

"I saw you on television," she said. "Your jacket looks like you stole it from Liberace. And you look three-hundred-years old."

"That figure's in the ballpark," I said. "I feel close to that."

"I know that," she snorted, turning her attention back to the televised adventures of Frontier Cretin. "Christ, do I ever know that."

Despite her steadily increasing drinking, Adele always managed to look twenty. Tops. She was thirty-seven but her face was so young and her body so young and every time she walked by me I remembered how much I had once loved her and how the booze had beaten and beaten at that love until it had curled up into a hard little ball, like an armadillo. It was a tightly packed little kernel but it was still there and maybe someday it would open up again.

Yeah, sure. When America reinstitutes Prohibition and she sobers up.

I cooked myself hash in the kitchen. Has anyone ever considered how many unhappy men the Broadcast Hash people have saved from starvation? I washed the dish and frying pan but I didn't dry them, because why do something that God has invented relative humidity to do. Then I went into the spare room that I used for a study. It would have been a bedroom for our baby but Adele could never have one. That's probably where things went bad, when we found out Adele's tubing was twisted, and some pig-faced social worker turned us down for an adoption because she didn't like cops.

I lay down on the couch and thought about Barry Dawson and the case and Leonardo and Drossner and Chief Semple and that if Adele and I were to split, I might just pack in the job and go somewhere and be a lumberjack.

Garbage. I wasn't so far gone that I couldn't recognize self-pitying bullshit. I love being a cop. They'd have to use a paint-scraper to pry me loose from the job. And for my marriage, I'd rather reconcile. Who knows? Maybe someday.

After a while, I turned on the small television set to watch the eleven o'clock news. Through some judicious juggling and some accommodating schedule-making by the news shows, I was able to get the Dawson story on two channels and half of it on another channel.

I wasn't on any of them.

By this hour, all the news was Drossner, impeccably tailored, strikingly articulate, insufferably arrogant, outlining all the details of the insoluble murder mystery. Barry Dawson's greatest mystery. The Master Puzzler's final gambit. I swear to God he said things like that. He could make a living moonlighting writing headlines for the *National Star*.

They got the facts pretty straight, at least for television, but on the half-story that I saw, there was something I'd been waiting for. A reporter said sources close to the investigation disclosed that an arrest might be made within twenty-four hours.

That was Drossner talking to somebody. Whenever a story mentions a source close to the investigation, article of faith, that source is the person running the investigation, who just doesn't want to be quoted yet. It's always a top cop or a state's attorney. The only other people close to an investigation are slogging foot-soldier cops and they don't talk to reporters at all because they know the bastards'll hand them up in an instant.

That wasn't all that was disturbing about the TV coverage. I didn't mind not being on but Chief Semple wasn't on either. I'd hear about that tomorrow.

And with that pleasant thought, I fell asleep on the naugahyde couch with the four cigarette holes. Adele would sleep on her couch out in the living room, with the television flickering all night. For all its use to us, the conjugal bed could go right back to the second-floor discount department at Klein's furniture store.

I don't know exactly what time it was I was awakened, but it must have been pretty late because the television was on with no picture, just illuminating the room like a phosphorescent glow from the mouth of a small cave. The telephone was ringing.

"Hello."

It was Leonardo.

"Anthony, I have finished the Dawson books."

His voice was as alert and sharp as if he were a championship fighter waiting in his corner for the bell to start round one.

"Yeah," I said. "Good. So?"

"Yes, I read the Dawson books. One thing we may be sure of is that Dawson did not use the tie-tack as a dying act to implicate his killer."

"How can we be sure of that?" I was finally starting to be able to speak English.

"These ten books are the worst kind of drivel. They contain forty-nine errors in logic—substantial, major errors. In addition, the errors increase with the newness of the books. He started out slipshod and careless and grew more slipshod and careless with each successive book. He simply was not smart enough or well-ordered enough to think of trapping Mr. Needles or anyone else with the tie-tack."

"I'm glad for you."

"I woke you," Leonardo said, obviously realizing for the first time that like most people I sleep during the night.

"That's all right. I was going to get up in a week anyway."

"I am sorry for waking you but I felt this was important."

"It is and I'm sorry to be feisty. Things don't always go well around here."

"You should get up from the couch where you lay,

pick Adele up in your arms and carry her into your bed."

"How do you know I'm lying on the couch?"

"I can hear the cheap plastic squeaking over the telephone as you move. Tomorrow we must look at the Dawson studio again. We must find out how this crime was committed. Because without that, we cannot prove who did it. There are many suspects."

"There sure are. Christabella, Barkmore, Payton . . ." I was going to keep going with my list but he interrupted to say again: "There are many suspects. We meet at the studio in the morning?"

"Sure."

"Eight o'clock?"

"All right."

"Fine," Leonardo said. "Sleep well. I will see you at eight. Oh, I went to the Golden Palace Restaurant tonight. Alfred Needles ate dinner there last night. He came in shortly after seven o'clock. He was the third customer for a waiter whose shift begins at seven o'clock. Give serious consideration to what I said about Adele."

"I will. Good night."

But I didn't. I just went back to sleep where I was.

CHAPTER NINE

They tell you that for mental health you ought to start off each day with a smile.

I didn't think I was going to do that when I got up and *The New York Times* and the *Walton News* were on my doorstep. They both had the stories, pretty much the same way television had had them the night before. All Inspector Drossner, all the insolubility of the crime.

No smiles there.

Adele was still sleeping it off on the couch. So I had coffee, brewed myself, and toast, burned myself. Still no smiles.

And then my phone rang.

It was Chief Semple.

"Did you see the papers, Jezail?"

"Yes, Chief."

"Goddam Drossner is getting all the coverage. Why is that?"

"Technically, he's in charge of the investigation, Chief."

Sometimes I felt like Sisyphus, spending my time in hell by trying to roll the rock of reason up the steeply sloped forehead of Chief Semple.

"Yeah, but I'm the chief of police."

"That you are. And no one better make any mistake about it."

"Damn right," he said. "But I'm not getting no coverage at all."

"I think it's a shame, Chief. I think the people deserved this chance to see their police chief in action."

"You're right, Jezail. I wouldn't be surprised if Drossner is duking those guys from the press."

"You never know, Chief. Ten bucks slipped into the right pocket and you could have *The New York Times* eating out of your hand."

"You're right, Jezail. I know what I've got to do."

"What's that, Chief?" I asked. I had several suggestions. He might learn to count. Perhaps offer himself up as a test subject to researchers into right-hemisphere/left-hemisphere brain behavior. How a man behaves with no brain at all. "What's that?" I asked again, in case he'd forgotten what we were talking about. I took a sip of my execrable coffee.

"I've got to solve this fucking murder."

I spit the coffee out on my toast, which helped soften it for later.

"That's the ticket, Chief," I finally managed to sputter.

"I'll talk to you later, Jezail. I've got to figure this out."

He hung up.

Smile? I started the day with a fit of laughter. I sat at the table and whooped uncontrollably. It roused Adele and she padded into the kitchen on marshmallow feet.

"What the hell are you laughing about?" she said.

"Chief Semple."

"At least he's the chief," she said, and she scuffed away to go into the bedroom to sleep till noon. So much for reconciliation. I stopped laughing and left the house. In five minutes she'd be out of the bedroom to fight and I didn't want any of it. The only thing worse than Adele drunk is Adele hung over.

I stopped in the center of town and dropped off my ripped jacket to be repaired, sliding it into the dry-cleaning chute along with a note to the tailor. I checked my office, then I drove down to the Dawson house. Leonardo's Cord was already there at the top of the walkway leading from the lot down to the studio.

He was leaning on the cyclone fencing, his eyes squinting, looking toward the waters of Long Island Sound, which separated Walton from the north shore of Long Island. He looked like a statue standing there. It didn't seem right to intrude on his private reverie with words so I just stood beside him. He did not acknowledge my presence with a greeting, but just began to talk.

"Knowledge is so mutable. Atoms were once

thought to be indivisible. And now we live in a world of subatomic particles, discovered faster than scientists can study them. We were brought up in a concrete world of three dimensions of length and height and breadth. All, we have been taught, must be reckoned within those three dimensions. And now we learn that there is a world of fractal, partial dimensions. This coastline itself has a dimension of one-and-a-fifth. And there are others.

"We have lived so many lives, learning so many things. Still there are so many things yet to learn."

He looked out over the water, his eyes, as they so often did, seeming to fix on a spot as if to overwhelm it with the power and intensity of his vision, and then he came to, snapping out of it by himself and turned to me with a smile.

"Enough reflection for one day, Anthony. Today we are interested in quite another dimension. The greatest and deepest of them all. The human mind."

"No, we're not," I said.

"No?" He seemed surprised.

"No. We're thinking of Drossner. What has that got to do with a human mind?"

His musical laugh seemed to spread out over the land and hang over the ugly building that was the Dawson studio.

"Hear, hear, Anthony. Hear, hear."

We ducked under the Police—Keep Out sign strung across the open gate and went down the stone steps to the studio. Patrolman Jackson was sitting on a small stone bench alongside the house near the window we had broken to get in to Dawson's body. We had posted a round-the-clock guard at the building to keep away sightseers, souvenir hunters, body-humpers, reporters, and other ghouls.

Jackson waved. "Hiya, Tony. Morning, Professor."

"Hello, officer," Leonardo said.

"How's it going?"

"I just came on," Jackson said. "Tracy was here during the night. Said it was as quiet as a tomb." He fingered the walkie-talkie on his hip.

"Door unlocked?"

He nodded.

Leonardo and I walked down to the end of the building and through the red Chinese door with the huge brass lockplate on it. The big portion of the building was cool and kind of shaded. The early morning sun was now behind the end of the building where Dawson's office was located. This part of the building got indirect light only, from a few windows on either side.

Gunter Wilke's tool box was placed neatly against the wall near the sink. The kitchen installation wasn't finished yet, but you'd never have known it by the looks of the work area. It looked as if a platoon of maids had just been in scrubbing the area and sucking up the sawdust.

Damned neat, those Germans. I know, I know, that's one of those nasty generalizations whose only redeeming virtue is its proximity to total truth. Screw it. The frigging Nazis are neat.

The big wooden door to Dawson's office was closed

and, in the dim light, it seemed to suck us toward it like a magnet. It was, of course, unlocked. It only locked by key from the inside and that key was now in the fine, Teutonic hands of Inspector Drossner. He was neat, too, come to think of it.

This was going to be my day for hating the neat. I have days when I hate blacks, Jews, Arabs, Chinese, all Orientals, women, firemen, and politicians. Today I hated neat. No rocks. Straight up.

Leonardo was safe. He was wearing brushed-denim brown levis, a yellow sports shirt, and had a white sweater tied around his shoulders. He had penny loafers on his feet. He was kind of neat but not well-dressed enough to hate.

He led the way into Dawson's studio. With windows on three sides, the room was bright and airy. The morning sun pouring in the windows behind the desk splashed brightly on the brown desk blotter, on the white desk telephone installed yesterday after Dawson's murder. Sorry, folks, can't come to the phone right now because I'm dead.

I wondered whom they would send the installation bill to. The phone company is inexorable. I hated them today, too.

Leonardo immediately began walking around the room, pressing his hands to the walls, feeling them from as high as he could reach, down to the floor. I sat down behind Dawson's desk. It was the closest I'd ever get to half a million dollars a year. I hated the rich today, too.

His back to me, Leonardo began to talk. "If

Dawson's death had occurred the way Inspector Drossner believes it did, we would have no riddle. He was beaten and, dying, with a clue to his murderer in his hand, he locked the door to his studio and then expired, simply to let us know that the evidence against his killer was airtight and tamper-proof. And Mr. Needles would be the killer. But we know that the final minutes of Barry Dawson's life did not happen that way because Mr. Needles is not the killer."

"You know that. I don't."

"Trust me, Anthony, it is so."

"I know. Because the television set was too blue."

"And because his cuffs had nothing in them. Remember that. And there are other reasons, too."

I grunted. He was running his fingertips over the wall paneling, as if looking for a hidden button that would trigger a secret panel.

"So what we have is this: Since Mr. Needles did not kill Barry Dawson, the locked room mystery did not occur Drossner's way. Somehow, someone else killed Barry Dawson and then managed to be outside this room with Dawson's body locked inside it."

"Suppose somebody just killed Dawson," I suggested, "and then ran like hell. And Dawson, dying, locked the door before he dropped. Just to keep the sonofabitch from coming back? Wouldn't that fill the bill?"

"No." Leonardo was now working his way along the far wall, past the door. "If Dawson had had strength and mind enough to lock the door, he would have had strength and mind to open the door and try to summon help. That is only logical. Perhaps he was confused. Perhaps he locked the door instead of opening it. Perhaps his befuddled mind and damaged body could not function correctly. Still he knew his salvation was the door. He would have stayed there until he collapsed. His body would have been found at the door, not eight feet inside the room."

He was on his knees now, running his hands along the molding at the bottom of the wall panels.

"But that is all conjecture," he said. "The hammer is much more definitive. If a killer simply struck down Barry Dawson, how would Dawson's fingerprints have gotten on the hammer? It is conceivable—barely likely, but conceivable—that a killer could have fled with the murder weapon in his hand. Then, in a moment of panic, realizing he still had it, he threw it away. That is logical. But would he have come back to put Barry Dawson's fingerprints on it? If he had, he would have found the door locked. Would he have put Dawson's fingerprints on it before he fled? If so, then we are not talking about a killer operating in a state of emotional panic. If he simply threw the hammer away to be rid of it, would he have thrown it only a few feet from the walk where it was certain to be found?"

"So many ifs," I said.

"Life is a collection of ifs," Leonardo answered. "We go from the buts of doubting childhood to the ands of accumulating knowledge, and finally to the ifs of questioning wisdom. No, there is only one answer that covers all those ifs. Someone killed Barry Dawson and arrogantly set a puzzle for the police to solve. In the process, he found a way to implicate Alfred Needles in the death. And in doing all this, he found a way to leave Dawson's body in this locked room and to make his escape. Ingenious."

"I'm impressed," I said. "So what are you doing now?"

"We have a classic locked room mystery. The first thing we must do is ascertain that there are no secret panels in this room, no unseen means of escape. If there were, it would, of course, implicate the builder, Wilke."

Leonardo was now examining the wall to my right. He moved quickly along the walls now, finishing behind me, and stood up and said:

"But there is none. I did not think there would be but one can never afford to overlook the obvious. It was the same with powered flight. We spent so much time trying to design flying machines, trying different techniques, different modes. But in reality, the solution to the problem was simply the design of an engine with a more efficient power-to-weight ratio. That is what made flight possible. And we missed it."

"We?" I asked.

"Mankind, of course," he said. "In the literature on the subject, there are really only four major types of locked room mysteries."

"There's literature on this?"

"Yes. Much has been written. The definitive work is the lecture by Dr. Gideon Fell."*

"Of course," I said. "Doctor Fell." I needed a cup of coffee. I went to the broken window and tossed Jackson my car keys. "Go get us some coffee, will you? Take my car. I'll be here till you get back. Leonardo, you want anything?"

"Milk laced with honey. Can that be arranged?"

"Jackson's a good man. He can do anything. Milk and honey, Jax?"

He shrugged at me. "I'll try. Coffee BNS?"

"Right."

"Be back soon," he said.

"I'm sorry," I said to Leonardo. "You were saying?"

"Four major types of locked room mysteries. More precisely, murders apparently committed in a hermetically sealed chamber." He went over and sat on the carpeted floor, his back against the wall near the door.

"The first type is the crime committed in a room that is really sealed. The murderer was never in the room. This can be an accident that looks like a murder. Most usually, a piece of furniture is the murder weapon. Or the victim kills himself either intentionally or accidentally after he is made insane by a gas or a drug. Or there is murder committed with a mechanical device. A tricked-up telephone, a clock with a booby trap in it. Any such device.

*John Dickson Carr, *The Three Coffins*. New York, Harper, 1935.

"There have been cases in which the death was suicide. A man shoots himself with a gun fastened to a string. The string goes up through the chimney and has a weight on the other end. The man fires and the gun vanishes, pulled up the chimney by the weight."

"Scratch that one," I said. "No chimney in this room."

"We may scratch all those prospects. They are rendered useless by the fact that we have the obvious murder weapon. It was found outside the room. No strings attached."

He looked around the room again and up at the ceiling, painted with sand-texture paint and decorated with wooden beams matching the oak of the wall paneling.

"We can eliminate the obvious absurdities. A bullet made of ice or frozen blood so it could not be detected. An arrow carved from an icicle. They are not pertinent here." He brought his hands in front of him and stared at the backs of his fingers.

"Another alternative is the murder committed from outside on a victim inside, using a thin blade passed between the panels of a wall. But that did not happen, because of the nature of Dawson's death." Looking around, he said, "It could not have anyway. Mr. Wilke seems too meticulous a craftsman to go leaving holes in his walls for swords to come through."

I perched on the edge of the desk and tried not to think of Wilke's wonderful craftsmanship and my seventy-five-dollar sports jacket with the ripped sleeve.

"So those ways do not work. They are insufficient

to explain the problem. Then we have windows that have been gimmicked to lock themselves after a murderer leaves. These have not been. Another common way is to remove a pane of glass, reach one's arm through, lock the window, and then simply replace the pane of glass with fresh putty. I checked these windows yesterday and that had not been done. Yes. The windows are excluded."

Leonardo jumped to his feet and went to the three-inch thick wooden door. When he was intent on something, he reminded me of some jungle animal, inspecting its fallen victim, almost daring it to move before he devours it.

"The third method is with doors and locks," he said, running his fingers over the hinges of the door, then opening it wide and swinging it shut. "The ways of attaching a string or lever to a key and using it to lock the door, and then removing the string, are virtually beyond counting. But here that method was not used because the key was not left in the door by artifice of the murderer but was firmly in the dead hand of Barry Dawson. The other major way is removing the pins from the hinges of the door, without disturbing the lock. But this door, as you can see, is hinged on the inside. That method would allow the killer to escape from this room only if the hinges were on the outside."

He turned to me. It would be wrong to say his face looked puzzled, but it had that expression it usually gets when he is about to drift off into some world of mind that he and he alone is free to enter. The look represented only an aspect of mind, but watching Leonardo, the change seemed to be a physical act, full of power.

I didn't want to lose him yet. "That's three ways," I said quickly. "You said there were four major methods."

He came back to me. "The fourth is deception and illusion. The key is found in Barry Dawson's hand. But it was not there until the murderer, the first to find the body, puts it there. If that were true, it would make you the murderer since you found the key. Are you guilty?"

"I'll cop a plea right now if it'll solve this damn thing."

"That shouldn't be necessary but I will keep your offer on file. The other suspect would be Patrolman Jackson as the first to have access to the body. Another deceit is for the first man on the scene to find the apparent victim, but the victim has not yet been killed. The first man is the murderer and he strikes the fatal blow. Again, that would be Patrolman Jackson. Fortunately, he has been cleared by the autopsy report, which made Mr. Dawson dead for some sixteen hours before he was found."

At that moment, Jackson stuck his head back in the window. "Got your coffee, Tony. And your milk and honey."

"Thanks, Jax," I said. "You'll be glad to know the professor just cleared you of Dawson's murder."

"I didn't even know I was a suspect," he said with a casual grin. He handed the containers in through the window and gave me back my keys. I gave him a dollar to cover the cost.

Leonardo sipped at his golden milk and honey. "So those are the four major ways of perpetrating a locked room mystery. Of course, each of those breaks down into a number of subspecies. I believe there are fifty-seven in all. But they are all parts of the main four."

"And none of them solves our problem," I complained.

He looked jubilant. "I know," he said. "It is marvelous, isn't it? A new sealed room puzzle to solve."

He walked to the window and looked out to Long Island Sound. "An ingenious riddle left for us to unravel." His voice began to drift, to trail off.

"If we can," I said.

"We will," he said, his voice dying and his body almost stiffening as he looked away out over the water.

The telephone rang.

It was Chief Semple.

"Jezail?" he said. "Good. Listen. I read all those reports on your desk." The thought of the chief pooching around my desk with his mitten fingers nauseated me but I kept still.

"Yes?"

"Well, that tie-tack belonged to Needles. I think he killed Dawson."

"I think Inspector Drossner feels that way too, Chief," I said.

"So what do you think?"

"About what?"

"Should I leak it to the press? That Needles is the killer?"

I could just see Chief Semple's idea of leaking a story. It would involve mimeographing a misspelled press release and standing in front of police headquarters, roaring it out at the top of his lungs. I would have loved to have seen him do it but organizational loyalty made a coward of me.

"No, Chief, I don't think so."

"Why not?" His voice narrowed its range. I could hear suspicion leaking out of the telephone earpiece.

"Two reasons, Chief." Being with Leonardo always made me think logically and sequentially. "First. If you leak the story, you won't get any credit for the solution of the crime so there's no point in leaking it. Second, it's just possible that Needles isn't guilty, in which case the whole department might wind up having egg on its face."

He was silent, thinking about that.

"Who do *you* think killed Dawson? Maybe I can leak that? Is there still a chance it was a nigger? What does the fag say?"

"Sorry, Chief, I don't have a suspect yet. I just don't think it's Needles."

"Okay. But when you get a suspect, you let me know so I can leak it to the press. Get some headlines for the good old Walton P.D."

I had three or four headlines in mind. I could see them all. Hundred-and-forty-four-point type, the kind usually saved for a declaration of war. Printed in red. Ten times the usual number of papers printed and all distributed free. Delivered house to house. Blanket the world. Print some in Esperanto.

"POLICE CHIEF DECLARED INSANE."

"CHIEF SEMPLE COMMITTED AS HELPLESS WARD OF THE STATE."

"TOP COP BOOKED FOR EATING WORMS."

"POLICE CHIEF'S MIND QUALIFIES FOR AID TO UNDERDEVELOPED AREAS."

The telephone clicked in my ear before I could tell the chief any of my good headline ideas. The phone rang again as soon as I hung it up. It was my morning for retards.

Inspector Drossner said, "Jezail, I'll be going back to the Dawson house at . . ."

"At twelve-fifteen," I could not help interjecting.

"Oh. You've been notified already?"

"No. I just guessed."

"Er, well, I'll be up there at twelve-fifteen. We're going to wrap this thing up. Be there, will you?"

"We'll be there."

"We?"

"Leonardo and I."

"Oh, yeah. Bring him along. Let him see how the pros work." His intonation carefully included me among the pros so I resisted the impulse to tell him he was had found the wrong Needles in the haystack.

"I will. You're booking Needles?"

"Yes. The tie-tack should do it. Of course, keep that to yourself. I haven't told anybody yet. Especially the chief. I don't think he's too stable."

"I couldn't say," I said, being very politic.

"Wise man. See you later, old fellow."

Old fellow. What crap. The next thing, Drossner'd be wearing a deerstalker cap and carrying a magnifying glass.

I sipped my coffee slowly and quietly. It was ten minutes before Leonardo turned back from the window, his eyes bright and shining as if they were powered by batteries and he had just gotten a recharge by staring at the sound. He was chewing on a ball point pen.

"Chief Semple and Drossner," he said, more as a statement than a question.

I nodded. "Drossner will be at the Dawson house at twelve-fifteen. Score one for Professor Leonardo, the public relations expert."

He glanced at his watch, a pocket watch that he wore on a silver chain. The watch seemed to be as big as a travelling alarm clock and I guessed its weight at a pound and a half.

"It is nine o'clock," he said. "Let us go up to the main house now and see if we can speak to Alden Barkmore and Mrs. Dawson."

I dumped the coffee container into a wastepaper basket under Dawson's desk. The basket had been emptied the day before by my detectives but had contained only junk. Kleenex, scraps of paper, two advertisements from companies trying to sell luggage and a terra-cotta frying pan that made everyone a whiz at cooking steak in its own natural juices.

Leonardo carefully put the cap back on his empty

container of honeyed milk and left it on the window-sill.

The gate leading up to the main house was still tied back with a piece of rope. One of Drossner's men was sitting in a state police car just inside the main gate of the estate, presumably to keep the press hounds away from the grieving widow. He started to get out when he saw us, then recognized me and waved. I knew he would rethink that all very quickly and be on the radio to Drossner in a little while.

Alden Barkmore was on the lawn near one of the side entrances to the house. He was wearing one of those karate outfits, I think they call it a gi, but he was dancing. By himself.

"Check Battling Nijinsky," I said to Leonardo as we approached and watched Barkmore gently wave his arms around in the air, lift one leg at a time, then slide hoppingly from foot to foot. It was all like a slow-motion swat at a butterfly.

"Tai chi chuan," said Leonardo. "It started as a method of hand fighting in China, but over the centuries, its movements have become so stylized and so useless for fighting that it has developed the aspects of ballet. It is very good exercise, however. It gives one strength. Very good exercise."

"So is chewing tough liver," I said.

"Will you please go inside and see if you can find Mrs. Dawson and get answers to our questions? I will stay out here and speak to Mr. Barkmore," Leonardo said.

It was all right by me. I'd rather look at Christabella than Alden Barkmore, even if Barkmore did have longer eyelashes. When I let myself in through the side door, which was partially open, Barkmore had stopped prancing around and was talking with Leonardo.

CHAPTER TEN

I stood inside the doorway, listening. The house was still, that kind of special Saturday morning stillness most houses have before anyone is up. In this part of the country, it's generally associated with postmartini coma.

"Anybody home?" I called.

I heard nothing, not a sound, not a footfall, and then Walter Payton was standing in front of me, glaring. If I had been a burglar armed with less than a howitzer, I'd have dropped to my knees and surrendered on the spot.

"I'm Lieutenant Jezail," I said quickly. "I was here yesterday. Is Mrs. Dawson up?"

Payton relaxed. At least his big, sinewy hands, held a couple of inches away from his sides, seemed to unclench and drop against his hips.

"Yes, Lieutenant. Mrs. Dawson is having breakfast. Follow me, please."

He led me down the hall and to the right to the big sliding doors to the room where Drossner had played Hercule Poirot yesterday. He knocked and entered without waiting for an answer.

"Mrs. Dawson," he said. "Lieutenant Jezail is here."

I saw him nod and then step aside and motion me to go in. The doors slid closed behind me.

Christabella Dawson was sitting at a round table near the bay window. A silver coffee service was in front of her, along with a tray of toasted English muffins. She wore a white satin dressing gown, the kind with fur around the edges that always makes a woman look like a campy imitation of Susan Hayward. Her legs were crossed at the knees, but the dressing gown wasn't, so the legs protruded out quite beautifully in front of her. I must have been staring at her face for a moment.

"Come in, Lieutenant," she said. "Have some coffee."

"Thank you. I will," I said. Or anything else she was giving away.

She poured for me as I went and sat at the table. Despite her load-on yesterday, Christabella Dawson looked like money in the bank. She was fully made up, but even without the mascara and the eyeliner and the false eyelashes and the different shades of blush and base and lip gloss, she would have been something else. Her eyes were bright and sparkling. Oh, to be young again and be able to drink like that and look that good the next morning. Hell, to be able to look that good any morning.

She handed me a cup of coffee and pointed to the cream and sugar. "I ought to apologize for yesterday, Lieutenant. I hear I got smashed."

She pulled her dressing gown together in front of her chest. I wanted to tell her it wasn't really necessary because I wouldn't look.

I shrugged.

"You understand, I guess," she said. "It was just the shock of the whole day. The booze went through me like a dose of salts."

"Happens to the best of us," I said. Her gown slipped open again at the chest, but dammit, she was aware of it and pulled it closed again.

"That's nice of you to say. What can I do for you?"

"Just a minor point. I didn't see a statement from you to Inspector Drossner's men yesterday."

"I wasn't in any shape to give one."

"I figured. When you were talking to the inspector yesterday, you said you stayed over in New York the previous night."

She sipped her coffee and with her eyes over the cup, nodded to me.

"Where'd you stay?"

"With a friend."

"What friend?"

"Is that important?"

"Drossner will ask you," I said.

"He's coming back here around noontime. Is that what he's coming for?"

"Maybe," I lied. "He's got more questions to ask. But he'll definitely take a statement from you." The gown was opening more and more as her fingers fluttered around the table. I could see the round swell of her breasts, the deep cleavage. I'm not really a boobie man but I'd be willing to make an exception for Christabella Dawson.

She nodded unhappily. "I suppose he will."

"He will, Mrs. Dawson."

"Call me Christabella."

"He will, Christabella."

Then she didn't say anything. I sipped at my coffee to give her a chance to think. I was in no hurry. I stared at her breasts. She suddenly pulled the robe closed, so I looked out on the lawn. Leonardo was still there with Barkmore. He was helping Barkmore adjust his hands in that Chinese ballet he was doing. Leonardo was demonstrating, Barkmore was copying, and Leonardo was then adjusting Barkmore's hands to the precise position.

She nodded toward the bay window. "That little bastard did it, you know?"

"Barkmore?" I said. I must have sounded a little surprised. Barkmore just didn't fit in with the way Dawson was killed. I mean if he'd been killed by being gummed to death, I would have picked up Barkmore in a twink on general principles. But he didn't seem like the kind to go hammering in heads. Even if Leonardo said that practicing tai chi chuan gave a person strength.

"Don't look so surprised," she said. "I think he did it. I think he's been stealing Barry's money for years."

"I'm sure it'll all come out in the wash," I said. "Now about Thursday night and where you were."

Christabella paused, then said, "I was out getting laid."

That's always a sure way of getting my attention. It worked again.

"You've got to remember," she said. "Barry had slapped me around. I was pissed at him. I got out of here and went to New York and got my package on."

Fine, but it didn't answer the question.

"And?" I said.

"I picked up some guy in a First Avenue singles' bar and I went to a hotel with him and spent the night."

"Who was he?"

"Damned if I know," she said. "He was just something I picked up off the counter." She smiled.

I guess you can take the girl out of the chorus line but you can't take the chorus line out of the girl.

With the truth finally sharing the table with the coffee and the English muffins, she seemed to lose her nervousness. Her hands stopped fluttering and she went back to stuffing a big bite of muffin into her mouth. She chewed it thoroughly. Her eyes never left mine.

"You don't know his name?"

She shook her head. "He said Jim. But they all say Jim."

"What about the hotel?"

She swallowed the last bite.

"Lieutenant, when you live a life like me, all hotels start to melt together in your mind. All the same. A door, a key, a bed, a bathroom to throw up in later. Besides, I was bombed out of my frigging gourd. Is that Drossner going to ask me all about this?"

"Maybe. I don't know."

"Are you going to tell him to? I don't like that mother. I'd hate to have it get in the papers."

"I don't know any reason why I've got to tell him anything about it," I said.

She reached her hands across the table and put them down on top of mine.

"That's kind of you, Lieutenant. What the hell is your name anyway?"

"Jezail. Anthony Jezail."

"Well, Tony, that's kind of you. I remember kindnesses. Maybe because I get so few of them."

She squeezed my hands in hers. She moved her upper arms toward each other, pressing them against her upper sides. The motions squeezed her breasts together and the cleavage got deeper and darker, a very grand canyon to get lost in.

The body was grand but the judgment was lousy. Like I know I'm not the worst-looking guy in the world and not bad for my age, but I'm soured and nasty and charm schools lock their doors when they hear I'm in the neighborhood. So she didn't just fall in love with my warmth over English muffins. Especially with that crap about I-remember-kindnesses-because-I-get-so-few-of-them.

Somehow, I had never figured Christabella for a suspect before but I did now. If she'd say that to me, she was capable of anything. Let her try it on Drossner. Maybe he'd go for it.

No, he wouldn't. It wasn't in the state police manual.

"You believe me, don't you?" she said. "It's all the truth." She squeezed my hands again. I extricated them from hers and stood up. Her little act was annoying me.

"My father was a policeman. I remember something he used to say," I told her.

She looked at me, working her smile for all she could.

"What was that?"

I leaned closer to her. "He said 'I'm too old a cat to be screwed by a kitten.' So am I." I stepped back. "Thanks, Mrs. Dawson, for the coffee. I'll let myself out."

"Please do," she said coldly. When I'd gotten a few steps away, I heard her mumble, "Prick."

When I got outside, the *pas de deux* had stopped. Barkmore had gone somewhere, maybe to that great tippy-toe Valhalla in the sky and Leonardo was alone on the lawn, kneeling in the grass. He looked up as I approached. He was holding a blade of grass in his hand and he bit it gently.

"They use too much fertilizer on this grass. It makes it very green, but the taste is acid and the grass will not be hardy."

"I'll be sure to put that in my report," I said.

He did not look up. He was busy pulling blades of grass and rubbing his fingernail down their length as if to test the strength of their fibers.

"Alden Barkmore is a very interesting man," he said. "Barry Dawson's will left half his estate to Mrs. Dawson. If they battled as much as it seems, any changes Dawson might have planned in his will might have been to her detriment."

"That's a motive," I said.

"Yes. Unfortunately, Inspector Drossner will take the other side of the coin. The remaining half of Mr. Dawson's estate would have gone to Alfred Needles."

"So that's a motive for Needles."

"Yes. Although we have no reason to believe that Dawson and Needles were, in any way, on bad terms."

"Drossner won't care about that," I said. "Changing the will won't be important to him. Just the fact that Needles would inherit something on Dawson's death would be enough."

"Mr. Barkmore also spoke of Christabella. She spent much time away from this house and spent large sums of money."

"How does he know that?"

"The bills come to him as Dawson's business manager. He called the woman, I believe, a 'professional consumer. A consumer of time, a consumer of money, a consumer of air. Altogether worthless.' I believe that's the gist of what he said."

"She is not one of his favorite people, I take it."

"It is often the case," Leonardo said, "with feminine men and aggressively female women. I believe it is jealousy. Did you speak to her?"

Leonardo stood up and dropped the last few blades of grass from his hand. "Weak grass," he said. "It will be brown before fall. Did you speak to her?"

"Yes. She thinks Barkmore killed Dawson, and the night before last, she was out getting laid. Her words," I said.

"Anybody she knew?" he asked.

"As a matter of fact, no. A saloon pickup. Some First Avenue bar. A hotel room and wham, bam, thank you ma'am. Some of it was truth, some con."

Leonardo consulted his watch. "Good," he said. "We have time to spend before Inspector Drossner arrives for his afternoon performance, so let us walk, and you can tell me which was truth and which was con and how you knew the difference."

"My pleasure."

As we walked out the gates of the estate, Drossner's man eyed us suspiciously. He was young and could have used some sun. He was sucking on a toothpick.

I leaned in the car window.

"What'd the inspector say when you told him we were here?"

"Nothing," he answered, a little surprised.

"Not a thing?"

"He said he hoped you weren't going to screw things up."

"He doesn't need any help, sonny. Not from us."

I don't exercise much so I'm glad Leonardo was on a talking jag because I was puffing too hard to speak.

We plowed our way on foot through the hills, along dirt paths, all through the area surrounding the Brown Farms section.

Leonardo pointed out to me the stump of an old wine-glass elm that was standing in 1620. He showed me where the colonial settlers fought and routed the local Indians. He discoursed on Walton's early economy—shipping—and pointed out the sites of its first churches and first schools.

He told me more than I ever wanted to know about the local flora and fauna, ran me up a hill and told me about the thieves who were the first settlers of the town, then took my pulse and told me I was out of condition and should not exercise so hard that my pulse rate went above 125 per minute.

"At least not until you get your awful wreck of a body into some kind of condition."

"Let me rest, dammit, and I'll be fine."

"You rest by walking," he said. "We must get back now so as not to miss Inspector Drossner."

When we got back to the Dawson estate, Drossner had already arrived. So had Chief Semple and a string of press cars. Television men who look down their noses at cops were setting up their cameras talking to each other. Print reporters who look down their noses at television newsmen, until they are offered a TV job, were talking to each other. I look down my nose at all of them so I didn't talk to anybody.

Drossner's man had moved his car directly across the driveway to block any unauthorized auto from entering. We walked past him without saying hello and up the front steps of the house.

The guard had a couple of helpers with him, which was good because reporters are curiously witless things. If they have to wait five minutes, one of them gets the bright idea to scale the wall to get into the grounds. Not that it's going to do him any good to get into the grounds, not that it's going to get him an exclusive story. No. He climbs the wall because he saw somebody do it once in a 1930's movie about the press. Or he read about it in a book. No, scratch that. Today's reporters only read Mark Lane. They would have seen it in an old movie. They never seem to have understood that those old Hollywood reporters scaled the wall to get a story. These twerps scale the wall and then wait inside the wall for somebody to hand them a compass and a press release.

"INTREPID JOURNALIST SCALES WALL
  TO GET COPY OF PRESS RELEASE."

They're winners.

Today I hated the press too, but that wasn't just a function of my dark and dour Scotch-Irish mood. I always hate the press.

When we got into the drawing room, Chief Semple was helping himself to Christabella's scotch. Christabella had changed into a black linen suit for the occasion. She glared at me as I entered. She was standing at the table near the big bay windows, looking out over the yard.

Needles was wearing a rumpled blue suit, sitting on the couch, looking dejected. His face brightened when he saw us and Leonardo smiled at him. Barkmore, who must have brought enough changes of clothing to open a men's shop, if that's what you would call it, was wearing a white linen suit. He was on the other side of the room from Chief Semple, leaning against a wall so hard it seemed he was trying to burrow himself into it. The chief must have threatened him with arrest for public faggotry.

Drossner was sitting on the wooden bench in front of the grand piano, imperiously, wearing, would you believe, a TV blue shirt. He was ready for his grand Charlie-Chan-in-the-living-room moment. No one was talking when we entered.

The chief saw me.

"Jezail," he bellowed, establishing immediately that I was Jezail and he was the chief. Then he spilled some of the scotch, establishing also that he was a cretin. He didn't bother to blot it off the polished wood of the bar, even though there were napkins there. That established the fact that he was a slob.

There was no answer called for. The bellowed "Jezail" was not a greeting, nor the introduction to a sentence. It was just his way of announcing that I was his subordinate. He probably wanted me to go and shield him from view of the rest of the room so he could stuff the Dawson silver in his pockets.

Drossner looked at me too as if inviting me, with his eyes, to go stand by him.

Leonardo was looking at an oil painting on the wall. I stood alongside him.

"A terrible painting," he said. The oil was of a broken-down barn. Weeds grew around it and in the fore-ground of the picture was a rickety old split-rail fence.

"I kind of like it," I said.

"It is four inches too wide," he said. "If an artist cannot measure, can he do anything else?"

"The perspective is good," I offered.

"Yes. For Marvel Comics. All it needs to be an absolute disaster is for us to be handed cardboard eyeglasses with green and red cellophane lenses so we can see it in living three dimension with the fence jumping off the canvas to eat us. The oil paint mixture has too much extender in it. There is a slickness to it it should not have. I know something about faulty paints. Here the artist splattered paint and tried to cover it over and failed. Here, his brush technique was more suitable for putting paste on the back of wallpaper. Altogether execrable."

As he spoke, he kept jabbing at the painting with an index finger that looked angry.

I leaned close. I recognized the artist's name. He was very well known around Walton and had already had two major gallery shows in New York.

"A lot of people like his work," I said stubbornly.

"A lot of people think Michelangelo the greatest sculptor of all time," he said contemptuously, dismissing this artist, Michelangelo, and me, all in one sentence.

I don't know. I looked at the picture again. I still liked it, but it *was* probably four inches too wide.

I supposed we were waiting for somebody or something and then I realized that Walter Payton wasn't in the room. Just then, he came in and apologized to Drossner for being late.

Drossner ignored the apology and stood up.

"I have asked you all here so we can close the books on the mysterious and tragic death of Mr. Barry Dawson."

He paused for dramatic effect and looked around the room. All eyes were on him. Christabella had turned from the window and was leaning against the sill watching him. The sunlight bathed the outlines of her black suit in a soft gray haze and she looked like a men's magazine photograph shot with those Vaseline-slicked lenses to soften the image. She was a magnificent woman, I realized again as I looked at her, and I wished I hadn't bothered to tell her what my daddy had told me long ago.

Barkmore was still pressed against the wall, watching Drossner. Needles sat on the couch, head still down, but eyes glancing upward. Walter Payton stood inside the side door like a Pretorian guard, his long, knotty arm muscles bulging under this thin plaid shirt.

Only Chief Semple seemed to be looking away and his attention was necessarily focused on the difficulty of holding a glass of Chivas Regal in two hands without dropping it.

Behind me, Leonardo was also watching Drossner, who began to stalk the room like a caged tiger.

"From the beginning," he said, "the problem in this case has been how Mr. Dawson's body came to be found in that locked office. The door can be locked only from the inside. There was only one key. That key was found in Barry Dawson's clenched hand."

He was enjoying this. Every moronic, clichéd word of it was like music in the ears of Inspector Walter Drossner. I could tell.

"But that would indicate that Barry Dawson locked the door himself *after* the murderer left the room and tried unsuccessfully to hide the murder weapon, a hammer, from us.

"Why would Barry Dawson, dying, lock the door himself? Only one answer logically fits the facts of the case. Barry Dawson locked that door to make sure that the killer would be apprehended. Because he did not have only a key in his hand.

"In his hand, Barry Dawson also clutched an object that would definitely identify his killer. Mr. Dawson was a great puzzle expert, a genius of modern American letters. He knew that when we found the door locked, we would come to the realization that he locked it. And he locked it so the evidence in his hand would be conclusive and definitive."

He looked around the room with a gaze that was out of Significant Posturing, Semester One.

Everyone was paying attention except Chief Semple. He seemed to be looking down, probably wondering if those feet sticking out of his trouser legs were his. Especially since he didn't remember putting them on this morning.

"Conclusive and definitive," Drossner repeated.

"We have been through this case many times with the help of Lieutenant Jezail and Doctor Leonardo."

Chief Semple looked up when he heard my name, particularly since he hadn't bellowed it. "And Chief Semple," Drossner added quickly. "This is the only solution that logically fits all the circumstances.

"Mrs. Dawson. Gentlemen. We did not announce to you or to the press everything that we found in Barry Dawson's hand." Drossner reached into his jacket pocket and brought out the glassine envelope.

"This object was also held in Mr. Dawson's hand."

He took out the small tie-tack and walked forward to Alfred Needles.

"Mr. Needles. This is your tie-tack, isn't it?"

Needles looked at it, gulped, and then nodded his head in dumb, forlorn confusion.

Drossner stepped back. His voice dropped four notes. "Then I arrest you on suspicion of the murder of Barry Dawson. You have a right to remain silent. You have a right to be represented by counsel, and if you cannot afford counsel, the court will provide you with an attorney. You are advised that any statement you make may be used in a court of law against you."

"But I didn't do it," Needles cried out. The look on his face was one of pure anguish. Chief Semple took the horrified cry by Needles as a threat to kill us all, with more hammers, probably with hidden nigger accomplices, so he put down his scotch glass and reached for his gun.

Abandoning all caution, I walked into his line of fire and approached Needles.

"Easy," I told him. "If you're innocent, there'll be plenty of time to establish it." I put a hand on his shoulder in what I hoped was a reassuring gesture. He recoiled as if the long arm of the law was getting ready to grab him and throw him into durance vile.

Drossner had backed away and, as if on cue, two of his men came through the sliding wooden doors. Quickly, they helped Needles to his feet, cuffed his hands behind his back, and looked to Drossner for orders.

"Take him down and book him," Dawson said. "For the murder of Barry Dawson."

The shock was beginning to lift in the room.

"He didn't do it," Christabella mumbled. "He couldn't kill a fly." She was probably holding out for Barkmore.

Barkmore said to Needles as he was being walked away, "Don't make any statements at all. I'll be right down to meet you." Not much question that he didn't believe in the image of Alfred-Needles-as-murderer either. I'm sure he was holding out for Christabella.

Walter Payton was shaking his head "no."

Chief Semple still didn't know what was going on but when he saw the mad dog hammer-killer Needles being led from the room, he holstered his gun.

I turned to look at Leonardo. He had turned his back on the room and was inspecting the oil painting again.

Drossner looked around the room for plaudits but got none. I tried to look noncommittal.

"Al was Barry's best friend," Barkmore said.

Payton nodded.

"Shit. I need a drink," Christabella said.

Drossner advanced on Leonardo and said, "I want to thank you for your help, Doctor."

Leonardo wheeled. "What help are you talking about?" he asked.

"You know, helping me to see the way this had to be. Don't you see? Dawson had to lock the door himself. The only reason would be to pin the murder on Needles."

He looked at Leonardo questioningly, as if searching his face for approval.

Leonardo said, "Your logic is impeccable." The room was hushed. Everyone was listening.

Drossner beamed with satisfaction.

"Your logic is impeccable," Leonardo repeated. "So is that of a man who says that if two is equal to three, then two plus two equals six. The logic is impeccable, but the answer is wrong. Two plus two equals four and you have arrested the wrong person."

"Then maybe *you* have the right person," Drossner said heatedly.

"Maybe I do," Leonardo said softly.

"Produce him," Drossner challenged.

"When I am certain."

"Talk's cheap," sneered Drossner. "It was Needles."

"Only time will tell whether you are right or I am right," Leonardo said.

"Time," Drossner said. "You amateurs can have all the time you want to play and make theories. But we have to do the work, to put it on the line, to make the hard decisions." He looked at me for reinforcement. I looked at Chief Semple. His gun had gotten stuck in

his belt on its way back to his holster. I backed away
a little bit so as not to get splattered with blood when
he shot himself in the foot.

Drossner turned to the chief. "Chief Semple, will
you come out with me to help announce our solution
to the press?"

Chief Semple acted as if someone had told him he
would get free all the groceries he could stuff in his
shopping cart in two minutes. He ran forward to go
outside with Drossner.

"Better leave the scotch glass here, Chief," I told
him.

"Right, Jezail," he said. He handed it to me.

Leonardo and I looked at each other. Barkmore
came up and asked, "Where will they take Alfred?"

"They'll book him at town police headquarters.
You know where it is?"

He nodded to me. "I want to be with him. I'll act as
his attorney for now."

Leonardo said softly to the nervous agent, "Please
tell Mr. Needles that there are those of us who know
of his innocence and will work to prove it. He should
not fear."

"I'll tell him," said Barkmore.

"And I will see you later?" asked Leonardo.

"Yes. As soon as I'm done."

The man still smelled of lilacs to me. He walked
away, past Walter Payton, and out the side door. Payton stood as if rooted, still shaking his head from side
to side, while Christabella poured herself a drink.

Leonardo and I stepped out into the front hallway.

The door to the porch was open slightly and we could see the flashing of strobe lights from photographers and Drossner's deep voice echoing into the hall.

"It is our belief that Mr. Dawson apprehended Needles while he was rifling the chest of drawers in the Dawson studio. They struggled and Needles hit his employer with a hammer that was left in the building."

Leonardo shook his head sadly.

"The man is a fool."

"I don't know. I don't have a better answer," I said.

"The differences between incorrect answers are only quantitative. Some are farther from correct than others. But the qualitative analysis of them all is the same. They are wrong. Incorrect. Mistaken. And so is this Drossner person."

"Why?" I asked.

He stared at me and his eyes were aflame. He seemed to be taking Drossner's opinions as a personal attack on himself.

"For twenty-seven separate reasons," he said. "But the hammer will suffice. Item. The hammer. Gunter Wilke told us it was missing from his tool box. How then did it get into Mr. Dawson's office so Needles could pick it up in a fit of rage when surprised in a burglary and beat his employer to death?

"Item. The hammer. Why, if he committed a murder in passion, did Needles carefully put Barry Dawson's fingerprints on the hammer? Remember. Mr. Dawson was not dead at this time either, according to Drossner's theory. So what did Alfred

Needles do? According to the inspector, he first beat Mr. Dawson's head in. Then, following some hastily concocted plot, he put Dawson's fingerprints on the hammer. Did he fail to notice then that Dawson was still alive, still breathing? If he was going to such great pains to cover up the murder he had just committed, would he not have hit Mr. Dawson again to make sure the murder was indeed a murder?

"Item. The hammer. Now Needles throws the hammer away. Is he doing it in frightened passion now or with cool calculation? We do not know. Does it matter? Why would he, for either reason, in either state of mind, throw the hammer a few feet away from the path so it would be easily found? There is no reason for that. Why would he throw it in the direction of the main house when that would simply throw suspicion on those who live in the main house? Including himself.

"There is no reason for Mr. Needles to act as Inspector Drossner states he acted. The murderer is someone else."

"What about the color television? What was that all about?" I finally got the question in.

"In the past three years, there have been at least four studies of how a person's psychological state manifests itself in that person's tuning of a color television set. Every one of those studies reaches the same general conclusion. Those who tune their sets to blue are people who are placid and in a restful state of mind. Can you conceive of Mr. Needles killing his employer and friend, then coming back and tuning his color television set to reflect a calm and untroubled mind? Of course not. The evidence there for Mr. Needles's innocence is not conclusive, but it is another thread in the man's mantle of innocence.

"And there is the question of Alfred Needles's dinner. Gunter Wilke said he left the studio when it was getting dark. Sunset today is at six-thirty-two. Suppose he left at six. Needles's television set was being delivered at that time. So he got his television set and adjusted it and watched it, then raced down to kill his employer, and then went to the Golden Palace Restaurant to eat. Last night, I went to the restaurant. They know Mr. Needles quite well and he dined there shortly after 7 p.m. on the night of the murder. When did he kill Barry Dawson?"

"Why did you say it was important that there was nothing in his cuffs?" I asked.

He took a ballpoint pen from the packet of them he carried in his shirt pocket. He put it in his mouth and chewed on the side of it.

"Think for a moment of the all-important tie-tack on which Inspector Drossner pins so much hope. According to his theory, the tie-tack was pulled off in a struggle between Mr. Dawson and his secretary. But tie-tacks are held onto ties by a clip, a little squeeze device fastened from the underside of the tie.

"If the tie-tack was torn off in a fight, where is the clip that must also have fallen off? I searched the Dawson studio as did you and your men. It was not there. All right. Presume it fell into Mr. Needles's clothes. Perhaps in the cuff of his trousers. I checked the clothes he was wearing the night Mr. Dawson was killed. If you will remember they were on the chair in Alfred Needles's room. There was no chip, not in the pockets, not in the cuffs. And there was none in his jewelry box. Did it just vanish after this violent fight between Needles and his employer? That is hardly likely. How much more reasonable to believe Mr. Needles's story—that he lost the clip several weeks ago and had not worn the tie-tack since, but instead, he put it into his jewelry box until he remembered to get a new clip for it. Remember, it is jeweled and it is valuable. How sensible to put it in the jewelry box so as not to lose it and how foolish is Inspector Dross-ner's explanation. The tack was quite obviously stolen from the jewelry box. All police officers should be made familiar with Occam's Razor."

"Whose razor?"

"Occam's Razor. It is a philosophical principle that says one should not multiply entities unnecessarily. In other words, one should not grope about seeking the most complicated possible solutions to problems, when there are usually much simpler and more common solutions to them. Do not postulate flying saucers when weather ballons are sufficient. I am going to introduce Inspector Drossner to Occam's Razor and . . ."

Leonardo paused, as if he had heard something.

"And?" I said.

"And cut his throat with it. I do not like that man." Without changing the tone of his voice, he added, "You may come out now, Walter."

As if he were being dragged, Walter Payton came

from around the corner of the corridor. He looked shamefaced.

"If you wish to listen to our conversation, you might more simply join us," Leonardo said. "Rather than eavesdrop."

"I'm sorry, Professor. I just wanted to hear what you were saying. But I want to tell you you're right. Alfred didn't kill Mr. Dawson."

"Who did?" I asked quickly.

He shook his head.

"I don't know, but Alfred didn't. He loved Mr. Dawson. Just like I did. He wouldn't do it. Please, both of you, you make that inspector see that."

"It will be our pleasure," Leonardo said. He stepped up and put his hand on Payton's shoulder. "And how is your mother?"

CHAPTER ELEVEN

Leonardo and I walked down to the Dawson studio, since our cars were parked in the lot on the other side.

Jackson was still sitting down on the bench next to the building and from inside we heard the sound of hammering. Jackson came up to meet us when he saw us coming.

"Who's inside?" I asked.

"The old guy, Wilke," he said. "He said it vuss no business uff hiss who inherits da house. He vuss paid to build the kitchen and build it he vill, by God."

"Your accent's awful," I said.

He looked chagrined. "I heard that Drossner was booking Needles. So I told him to go in and work. I didn't think it'd do any harm."

"I guess not."

I turned to look for Leonardo but he was gone

from my side. He was standing in the open doorway to the building, looking inside.

Gunter Wilke was inside mounting a cabinet over the sink. He used a nail punch to sink the nailheads below the surface of the wood, and then used a wax pencil he carried in the vest pocket of his coveralls to wipe on the wood, fill in the small indentation, and make the nail invisible. The job was almost done. A few more nails, some paint on the ceiling, and Wilke could get back to his Bund meeting.

"It is just a pleasure to watch a good and thorough craftsman," Leonardo said to me.

"Yeah. The last thing I made was a shoebox in junior high school. It took me three years and two hundred pounds of nails and screws and it fell apart while I was carrying it home."

"Your talent lies elsewhere," Leonardo said.

Wilke stopped working when he heard us talk. He put down his hammer and looked at us as if we were stepping on a freshly seeded lawn he'd been working on for a month.

"Doctor," he said in his thick accent. "Lieutenant."

I guess that was as close as he came to a polite greeting.

He babbled something in German and Leonardo answered him. They spoke for perhaps two minutes, back and forth, and I felt like an invisible man, with the world going on around me and no one taking any notice of my existence. I always feel that way when people are talking a foreign language around me. It spoils vacations for me because I always think the

damn foreigners are talking about me, telling jokes
about the stupid American, or making fun of my ridiculous shirt.

Leonardo said "Herr Needles" and Gunter Wilke
nodded as if Leonardo had just confirmed something
he had always known.

Then, without even a pretense of civility, Gunter
Wilke turned and began to hammer again at the cabinet.

Leonardo shrugged. "He was interested in the
case," he explained to me. "He also thinks Needles did
it."

"Doesn't everybody?"

"Not everybody," he said, laughing. "Not Mrs.
Dawson or Mr. Barkmore or Mr. Payton or you or
me."

I nodded. Before I could say anything, we heard a
voice behind me.

"Hi, Pop."

We turned. There was a young man standing in the
doorway looking at Wilke. Wilke turned around and
his voice seemed angry as he said, "What are you
doing here?"

"I brought you some beer for lunch," the young
man said. Then he stopped as he saw Leonardo and
me.

"Hello," Leonardo said. "I am Doctor Leonardo.
This is Lieutenant Jezail."

The young man was about thirty. He had blond,
theatrically tousled wavy hair and shoulders so square
that it looked as if shoulder boards were built into his

shirt. His face was well-tanned. He wore a light green denim leisure suit, with the sleeves of the jacket pushed up his thick forearms.

Wilke said, "This is my son. He has been sick but he comes to bring his father beer for lunch." Parental pride. It was hard to believe a human emotion from that nasty old man.

"Nice to meet you," the man said. He nodded to both of us and walked over to hand his father a paper bag. He was carrying a folded-up newspaper in his back pocket.

"Thank you," Wilke said. He took a bottle of beer from the bag, twisted off the cap, and then sat on the edge of the sink, next to a plastic bag. From it he took his sandwiches. Taystee bread is awful but the plastic bag it comes in is the greatest thing to carry sandwiches in.

What a great equalizer. I carry my sandwiches that way, Wilke carried his sandwiches that way, and if all the Rockefeller brothers carried their lunch to work, they'd carry them in Taystee bread bags with those little yellow wire fasteners twisted around the top.

"Now you go right home and get back to bed," Wilke said to his son.

"Okay, Pop." The young man turned and smiled at us, then glanced at his watch.

"And how are you doing in your jai-alai selections?" Leonardo asked him.

The young man looked surprised, then realized he had the paper in his back pocket. He took it out and looked at it. It was opened to the jai-alai morning line, and there were ink marks on the racing lists, noting his betting choices.

"So-so," he said. "You play, Doctor? It is Doctor, isn't it?"

"Yes. I play a little," Leonardo said. "I have had some success by mathematically combining Teams 1, 2, and 8, which win a preponderant number of games."

That was obviously a new system for young Wilke but before he could comment, old man Wilke's voice interrupted.

"Ernest, since you are going, please take this tarpaulin up and put it in the back of the truck. I will not need it for a while."

He pointed to a tarpaulin neatly folded on the floor near the wall.

"My master calls," young Wilke said with a grin. He went over and hoisted the thick canvas tarp to his shoulder and went back to the front door. "Nice meeting you both," he said. "So long, Pop." He looked at his watch again as he left.

Then he went out and there was no sound in the room except the chomping jaws of Gunter Wilke, biting into his sandwich of brown bread and what was unmistakably limburger cheese. Now I knew why he wrapped his sandwich so carefully in a plastic bag and sealed the top to make it air-tight. My grandfather used to eat limburger cheese. Its smell made me sick. It still does. I hated my grandfather. What kind of Scotsman eats limburger?

"Auf weidersehn," I ventured and headed for the

door to get some air. I didn't want to be impolite and throw up inside the house.

Leonardo followed me. He looked up to the open fence gate in the middle of the steps leading up to the main house.

Christabella Dawson was standing at the gate, looking down, her body nice and alive under that black pants suit. She was smiling.

Then she saw us.

Without acknowledging that she had, she turned and walked back up the steps.

"Maybe she just wanted to look at the place," I said.

"Maybe," said Leonardo.

I told Jackson there was no need for him to hang around any longer, and I would drive him back to headquarters. When we got up to the parking lot, a green Porsche, obviously Ernest Wilke's, was driving away.

The carpentry truck, labeled Wilke and Son, was parked next to my car too close, and I had to get in on the passenger's side.

I called across to Leonardo: "See you at headquarters."

He did not answer. He was standing next to his white Cord, looking off into the distance.

When I drove off with Jackson, I glanced into the rearview mirror. Leonardo still had not moved.

Jackson decided to eat lunch so I dropped him at a diner on the Post Road on my way back into town.

Then I stopped at the tailor's to pick up my ripped jacket.

He had done a good job on the torn sleeve and only charged me five dollars for the reweaving. Good price and fast service, and that's one of the tangible fringe benefits of being a policeman. I take them all. In the old days they used to steal apples and bananas from sidewalk fruit stands.

Walton police headquarters is in an old brick building that looks like a turn-of-the-century schoolhouse. There are never any parking spots around it, but everybody parks in a bank lot across the street. Leonardo's car was already in the parking lot and I eased into a spot next to him. Living in Walton has some advantages, like not being required to lock your car when you park it. But I had my repaired jacket in the car. Lock or not lock? Not lock. But I took my jacket with me.

Newspapermen were hovering around the front of police headquarters, the only one I've ever seen by the way that doesn't have the traditional green globe lights. We have blue lights, designed to look like kerosene lamps. Nothing is sacred around here.

When I got near the steps, Leonardo was coming out of the building with Alden Barkmore. They worked their way through the newspapermen quickly, Barkmore declining to say anything more than he had already said. They met me at the edge of the parking lot.

"Alfred Needles has been booked and fingerprinted and photographed," Leonardo told me. "Mr. Barkmore has been present and has told him to make no statements whatsoever. There will be an arraignment and a bail hearing tomorrow."

I nodded.

"We are now going to have a drink and to talk. Will you join us?"

"I'd better get inside and show my face," I said. "I'll meet you."

We agreed to meet at John Henry's, a walking-distance pub that's located in what used to be an ice cream parlor. At night, it's a singles' hangout and spending five minutes there after dark is like Walpurgisnacht. But in the daytime, it's kind of quiet and civilized.

I found Inspector Drossner in Chief Semple's office. They were reinforcing each other.

"Burglary, pure and simple," Drossner was saying as I came in. "And he got caught and hit Dawson with the hammer."

"That's the way I figure it, too," Chief Semple said.

I didn't say anything, so Semple asked me, "What do you think, Jezail?"

"I don't know yet."

"But the tie-tack," Drossner said. He seemed desperate to convince somebody of something. "What other explanation could there be?"

"A frame-up," I said. "Somebody trying to pin the killing on Needles."

He smiled at me patronizingly. I felt like a spastic who'd just hit himself in the forehead with his own ice cream cone.

"Doesn't work, Jezail. If somebody planted that tie-tack in Dawson's hand, then Dawson is already dead. So how does the killer get out of the locked room?"

"I don't have an answer to that one yet," I said.

"And you're not going to get one either," Drossner said positively. "The only one that works is mine. Are those reporters still outside?"

"Yeah."

"Well, maybe I ought to go out and talk to them. Send them on their way so we can get back to doing police work around here."

"Damn right," said the chief. "I'll go with you." He wasn't going to miss any ink if he could help it.

"And Jezail?"

"Yes, Chief."

"I'm tired of seeing that fag hanging around."

"You mean Doctor Leonardo?"

"You know any other fag who's hanging around here?"

"The First Selectman personally asked him to look into this case," I said.

"Well, the case is solved so he can stay away from now on."

"This Leonardo's an arrogant sort, isn't he?" Drossner asked me.

"Not really. He just thinks differently from ordinary people."

"He's a faggot," Chief Semple said.

To his credit, Drossner ignored that. "What's he after in this case?" he asked me.

"The truth. That's what he lives for."

"The truth," Semple exploded. "The truth is that we've got that frigging killer behind bars. That's the truth."

"Leonardo doesn't think Needles did it."

"Well, your precious Leonardo is wrong, sweets," Semple said. He came very close to getting punched in the face for that.

Drossner nodded.

"It was burglary," he said with finality.

"Why are you carrying that jacket around?" asked Chief Semple.

"In case it rains," I said. "I'll have a change to dry clothes."

Semple nodded as if that made sense. He was still nodding when he came from behind his desk to follow Drossner outside and pose for more pictures.

I checked in my office but nothing was happening so I went out a side door to miss Drossner and Semple and to go to John Henry's.

Leonardo and Barkmore were sitting at a table in the back of the saloon in front of leaded Tiffany glass panels that covered fluorescent lights. The inside of the place was wood and copper and around the top of the walls were plaques with famous and not so famous quotations, mostly about drinking.

"Work is the curse of the drinking classes."

"I can resist everything except temptation." Oscar Wilde.

Talk about your literary artsy-craftsy towns. A singles bar in which everybody is playing grab-ass, their

mind on just one thing, getting laid, and nailed to the
walls they have a condensed version of the Fifty Great
Books list.

Leonardo had wine and water in front of him, the
water tinted pink where he had poured wine into it.
Barkmore was sipping a drink that was green and
frothy and looked like a culture used to grow mara-
schino cherries.

I sat down next to Leonardo and set my jacket on
the seat between us. My knee touched Barkmore's under the table and I pulled it back quickly. I know all
that Freudian crap about protesting too much etcetera
and people who loudly hate homosexuals are latent
homosexuals themselves and blah, blah, blah, I know
all that and I'll take my chances. Those people just set
my nerves on edge. I'd rather spend ten centuries with
Anita Bryant than ten seconds with all the gay rights
loonies in the world.

"Alden is remaining here to represent Mr. Needles
until other legal arrangements can be made. Mr.
Needles has no family. so there will be no one to assist
him."

"Yes," Barkmore said. "I'm admitted to practice in
Connecticut. Some of my other clients live here and I
found it was just good policy to be able to handle everything of theirs. Wills, house closings, all that." He
smiled at me.

"Then you drew Dawson's will," I said.

He nodded.

"And he would have discussed with you any
changes he wanted to make."

"That's right," he said.

"But you're only presuming that Dawson wanted to talk to you about his will. Maybe he had something else on his mind."

I looked hard at Barkmore and he seemed to fidget in his seat. "Do I detect some suspicion on your part, Lieutenant?"

"Just doing my job," I said.

"Well, you can scratch me as a suspect," he said. "When Barry was killed, I was in California."

I nodded.

Leonardo said, "When you arrived, Anthony, we were discussing the relationship between Barry Dawson and his wife."

"Eminently and imminently splittable," Barkmore said.

"You think she killed him?" I asked.

"She's nasty enough to do it," Barkmore said. "But I don't think she's got the brains." He held his two hands cupped out in front of him, in imitation of Christabella's breasts.

Leonardo shook his head and sipped that awful mixture in his water glass.

"A very recent study shows that it is not true that women with big breasts are necessarily stupid," he demurred gently.

"She thinks you did it," I told Barkmore.

"She would," he said. "I don't know why she's jealous of me."

I did. She was annoyed that he had longer eyelashes than she did, but I didn't say anything.

I ordered a double Dewars on the rocks from the miniskirted waitress with the long blonde hair. They call her Tattoo and I don't know why but she keeps threatening to show me.

After she left, I told Leonardo, "This is some goddam case. We don't know who and we don't know why and we don't even know how."

"We will," he said. "We will."

"It wasn't Alfred," Barkmore said. "I know that. He was absolutely devoted to Barry. He might kill somebody *for* him, but he'd never kill him. In ten years, I never heard him say an unhappy thing about working for Barry. And I never heard Barry say anything bad about him."

"Well, somebody killed Dawson and Drossner thinks it was Needles caught red-handed in a burglary," I said.

"That is idiotic," Leonardo said. "We are going to New York." He asked Barkmore, "You will have that material?"

"I'll call my secretary. She'll be there waiting for you tonight."

"All right," Leonardo said. "Thank you."

"What material?" I asked.

"I'll tell you in the car. That is, if you are free to accompany me now."

I thought of Adele at home.

"I can go with you."

"Good. Then let us forget our problems and spice our drinks with the oil of pleasant conversation."

"Suits me," I said.

"Is that the jacket you tore?" Leonardo asked. "Has it been repaired satisfactorily?"

I handed it to him and pointed out where the hole in the sleeve had been.

"Very good," he said.

I noticed a sheet of yellow paper sticking from the pocket of the jacket. For a moment I thought it was the tailor's bill, then remembered it was the page I'd taken from Dawson's pad the day before.

I handed it to Leonardo.

"Here. I don't think you ever saw this."

He unfolded the paper and glanced at it.

"What is this?"

"It was on Dawson's desk. I put it in my pocket to stop the chief from doodling on it. Those scrawls in the corner are his."

Leonardo looked at it carefully, then pushed the sheet across the table to Barkmore.

"Is that Barry Dawson's handwriting?"

Barkmore looked at it, cleared his throat and read aloud:

> April Fifteenth.
> The sun lives and creates life.
> Master builder, it rides high and golden
> and turns the dull brown of dirt
> into the brightness of flowered fields.
> The sun dies and creates death,
> but in an imitation of life.
> The red ball sends its rays
> through colored glass,

splashing dagger-jagging flashes
of colored lights against dirt-colored
oaken panels that once also lived.
The sun's life is the color of gold.
The sun's death is the color of blood.
The sun is just like man.

Barkmore looked at Leonardo. "That's Barry's scrawl. And his poetry too. He always wanted to be a poet. Another comic wanting to do Hamlet."

"It is man's way," said Leonardo, "to wish to be what he is not." His face was lit up by an inner electricity. His voice sparked with tension. He took the sheet from Barkmore and read the poem again to himself.

"It is terrible poetry," he said. "Still it may be regarded as a memorable piece of writing."

"Not likely," Barkmore said. "Barry couldn't write poetry at all."

"The poetry is execrable," Leonardo agreed. "But that does not make the writing without value. Come, Anthony, New York calls. You hold this paper for safekeeping."

"I'm going to stay here awhile," Barkmore said.

"Fine," said Leonardo. "And we shall see you in the courtroom tomorrow morning when we free Alfred Needles."

As we left, I asked Leonardo, "How can you promise that?"

"We have to," he said. "Tomorrow is Sunday and I have to be back in class by Monday morning."

Leonardo said that it was important that we stop at his house before going to New York.

We drove there in separate cars and when I arrived, Leonardo's Cord was already parked next to his house. The front door was slightly ajar so I went in without knocking.

Leonardo was on the telephone. He nodded to me as I came in.

"I see," he said. "Jayna, you are as smart as you are beautiful. If that is possible."

He listened for a moment, then nodded to the telephone.

"I hope we can. I hope we can do that very soon," he said. "Be well."

When he replaced the receiver, he said "As you may remember, I have some friends in Hollywood. That was one of them. Alden Barkmore was indeed in business meetings there all day Thursday. Even with the time differential between the coasts, he would not have been able to get back here in time to murder Barry Dawson."

"So you *did* suspect the little twit," I said.

"I suspect everyone. And no one," he said. "I just gather information. And now I must make another call."

He dialed a ten-digit long-distance number, waited a moment, then said: "Dr. Curcio, please. This is Doctor Leonardo."

He waited another moment, and then began speaking rapid-fire Italian. I don't understand a word of it but it's a very musical language when it isn't being grunted by a barber.

It was a few minutes before he hung up with, *"Grazie, grazie, dottore."*

"And so much for Walter Payton," he told me. "On Thursday night, he was having dinner with his mother four hundred miles from here. Come. We go."

He walked toward the door.

"In Syracuse?" I asked.

"Yes."

"That was the hospital?"

"Yes. When Inspector Drossner asked Payton yesterday about his mother, Mr. Payton hesitated before answering that she was in a hospital in Syracuse. There is only one hospital in Syracuse that a person might be ashamed to admit he had a relative in."

"Oh?"

"Yes. A hospital for psychopaths. Mrs. Payton is a patient there."

Leonardo walked around to my car and got into the passenger's side.

As I got behind the wheel, I said, "What's she in for?"

"Homicide," he said. "She killed her husband with an axe."

CHAPTER TWELVE

I always take the Merritt Parkway when I drive to New York. It's narrower and slower-going and older than the Connecticut Turnpike and maybe because the scenery is beautiful, people seem to be more civilized when they're driving. So it increases my chances of staying alive.

We went in my car and Leonardo let me drive. He was silent during the trip. He sat in the far corner of the front seat, leaning against the door. From his shirt pocket, he took a small plastic sleeve filled with colored ballpoint pens and a small note pad, and he was either drawing or making notes.

I can always tell when I leave Connecticut and get into New York state. The Merritt is a smoothly paved road that you can go for miles on without hitting a single bump. And as soon as it crosses into New York and becomes the Hutchinson River Parkway, the roadway gets chopped up and thumpy, and three

miles later, you have the final proof you're in New
York because the shoulders of the roadway are lit-
tered with hubcaps and tire rims, sometimes fenders
and, occasionally an abandoned car. I swear to Christ,
sometimes I think New York is inhabited by a mon-
ster that never crosses state lines but hangs out in New
York, eating automobiles and vomiting the spare parts
out along the roadside.

I used to go to New York a lot. Adele and I liked
to go to the theater, with dinner first, some drinks after, and while it put a pinch on a police lieutenant's
salary, it was fun. But then it stopped being fun because every night would end the same way with nasty
arguments and Adele drunk and snoring in the front
seat on the way home, and angrily resisting my efforts
to wake her up and get her out of the car when we got
home.

Once I let her sleep in the car overnight. She was
still there in the morning when I got up and while I
was drinking my coffee, she finally came in, looked at
me with her cold, hating eyes and said, "First good
night's sleep I've had in months. For a change, I must
have enjoyed the company."

We stopped going to New York. We both started
sleeping on our couches.

As I drove over the Willis Avenue bridge, Leonardo looked up, gave me an address on Central Park
West near 94th Street, and went back to his doodling.

I had parked outside the address on Central Park
West for about three minutes before Leonardo
stopped working with his ballpoints, put his pad

back in his pocket, and asked me to wait for him.

He darted through traffic across the street and went into a big, dingy gray apartment building. He was back down in ten minutes, carrying a thick envelope and a Manhattan telephone directory.

In the car, he took a pile of receipts from the envelope.

"These are Mrs. Dawson's charge bills for the last two months," he said. The pile was an inch-and-a-half thick. "All such bills come to Alden Barkmore for payment. Fortunately, he has all these receipts filed."

"And just what are you looking for?"

"I view with some suspicion Mrs. Dawson's tale of where she was and what she did the night her husband was killed. I do not believe that such a woman went to a First Avenue bar to pick up a man. I do not believe that she slept with a stranger she did not know in a hotel she does not remember. I believe she lied, and we are going to visit the restaurants she frequents to test this belief of mine."

Swiftly, Leonardo was separating the stacks of bills into a half-dozen piles, one for each restaurant and watering hole Christabella Dawson hung out in.

He looked up the addresses of the places in the telephone book and jotted them down on top of each stack of bills.

"One can tell by the amounts of the bills that Christabella Dawson rarely eats or drinks alone," he said. "And she goes out very frequently. Let us be off." He gave me an address on East 68th Street.

The restaurant was a dingy French dump, the kind

that has a resurgence every five years when a new crowd of suckers decides that dirty and tacky is really "with it."

I stopped in front of the place under a ripped, tattered canopy and Leonardo hopped out of the car and went inside.

He was back out in a few minutes, holding his stack of charge receipts for that restaurant. He was smiling.

"Mrs. Dawson did not eat there Thursday night. But she often dines there. And never alone."

"Male company or female company," I asked.

"Male. And recently, always the same male."

He handed me his small notebook. He had drawn two pictures on the paper with his ballpoint pens. The lines were precise and smooth, even though he had done it in the car riding down the highway. The drawings were so perfect they could have been engravings from U.S. currency, but the colors were camera-sharp and lifelike.

On the left was a drawing of Christabella Dawson. And on the right, a drawing of Ernest Wilke, Gunter Wilke's tousle-haired, sensuous-lipped son.

"I'll be damned. So they're a thing."

He nodded and took back the pad.

"Let us try this one next," he said and gave me an address on East 59th Street. It was an Italian restaurant, also seedy and dumpy, and if I didn't know better, I would have sworn they moved the French restaurant we had just left, and transported it down nine blocks while we weren't looking. The restaurant awning was ripped and tattered, the place dingy and dark. Leonardo was inside only a moment before reappearing.

"They know Mrs. Dawson very well. But she was not there Thursday night."

"Look. You know that she's running around with young Wilke. Why are you trying to pin down where she was on Thursday night?"

"Because Thursday night was the murder night. If we can show that Mrs. Dawson lied about her where-abouts and whom she was with, we then have reason to ask why did she lie. She certainly did not do it to protect her wifely honor, not when she told you that she picked up a man and spent the night with him in an unknown hotel. If she was with young Wilke on Thursday night, she lied, and lied for a reason. That reason will bear on Barry Dawson's murder."

We hit paydirt on the fourth restaurant, which was between Park and Madison in the Thirties. Even from outside, it was noisy and through the dirty window I could see the flashing of disco strobe lights. It gave its name as Le Bon Fils, the Good Son, and if a French name goes with Rumanian cooking and disco music, I'll kiss a duck. But this was New York and there's no limit to how people will let themselves be taken.

Leonardo was inside for five minutes. Presumably, his Rumainian isn't as fluent as his French or Italian. Or maybe they spoke only disco. Ya-da-da-da-da, love me, love me, love me. Ya-da-da-da-da, ooooooh, ya gotta love me.

When Leonardo came out, he looked satisfied. He

stood in front of the restaurant, glancing up and down the street, then came to the driver's window of my car.

"Anthony, please lend me your badge."

I fished my tin from my inside jacket pocket and gave it to him.

"I will be back promptly."

He trotted quickly across the street and down the block. I saw where he was going—The Duncan Arms.

It was a small hotel in mid-block. There was a slot at the curb in front of it so I drove over there to wait. I lit a cigarette and Leonardo was back before I had even begun to enjoy it.

"As you say—bingo," he said, sliding into the car and handing me back my badge. "Back to Walton."

"What'd you find?"

"A register with the name of Mr. and Mrs. Ernest Wilke on it. For Thursday night. A clerk who remembers that Mrs. Wilke was a beautiful blond whom he recognizes from my modest sketch. Mrs. Dawson and Wilke ate dinner and went to this nearby hotel and spent Thursday night here."

"Bingo," I said. "You're right. You think they killed Dawson?"

"I have not determined that yet."

"Seems likely," I said. "And we're moving. A little while ago, we didn't know the who or the why or the how. Now at least we're getting close to the who."

Leonardo looked at me quizzically.

"Anthony," he said softly. "You are mistaken. We already know the how. Back to Walton, please."

Within three minutes, he was asleep.

CHAPTER THIRTEEN

The courtroom on the second floor of the Walton Town Hall seats eighty-nine people. It isn't generally used since Connecticut integrated the court system and most cases, even routine traffic cases, go before the state courts in cities like Bridgeport and Norwalk.

It is stupid and inefficient not having real working municipal courts, but the politicians have claimed for so many years that it's intelligent, efficient, far-reaching, and economical that people believe them. Until they get a speeding ticket and have to drive thirty miles to court, miss a day's pay while they wait for six hours in a courtroom for muggers, rapists, armed robbers to go first, and then in twenty seconds, stand up, plead guilty, and pay a fifteen-dollar fine.

This Sunday morning, for the arraignment of Alfred Needles, Judge Eugene Willis from the Norwalk court came down to sit in our courtroom. He probably forgot what a real courtroom looks like. Ours is big with murals and a high ceiling and a big, mahogany judge's bench. The courtroom in Norwalk is new and it looks like an operating room.

All eighty-nine seats in the Walton court were going to be filled up for the arraignment of Alfred Needles. In the halls outside the court, TV photographers had set up their gear and newspaper photographers were roaming back and forth, telling each other their filthy jokes, and goosing young woman reporters. Really, if I were the photo editor on a daily newspaper, I think I'd wear disposable gloves. All the time.

Court was supposed to start at ten a.m. and I got there at about ten minutes till, wearing my freshly-repaired sports jacket. Drossner saw me in the hallway and excused himself from a reporter.

"Your friend, the professor, is he going to be here?"

"He said he would."

"I want him to. I don't want him to miss it." His anticipation was almost obscene.

"You sound like you're loaded for bear, Drossner."

"You remember your friend, how little he thinks of my burglary theory. Well, I've got a surprise for him and I just don't want him to miss it."

"He won't miss it," I said. And I couldn't resist. "He might have a surprise for you, too."

He turned cautious. "Oh? What's that?"

I shrugged. "Leonardo never tells me anything," I said. "Drossner," I continued, "I have a question for you."

"What's that?"

"How did you get a Sunday court session? How did you get a judge to sit on Sunday? That's like finding a doctor on Wednesday. Harder even."

"Well, Judge Willis is a very diligent judge."

So much for trying to make pleasant small talk with Drossner.

While we were standing there, Mrs. Dawson arrived with Walter Payton, who had somewhere found a too-small blue suit to wear instead of overalls. Not that anyone saw him much. Christabella was wearing a black dress and a veil, but even in mourning, she was some kind of good-looking woman and the photographers flashed a barrage of bulbs at her until she got inside the courtroom where they weren't allowed to follow.

Drossner drifted away because neither of us was much at small talk and I waited for Leonardo alone, smoking a cigarette. At two minutes to ten, I went inside. The first two rows had been reserved for officials and for potential witnesses. Mrs. Dawson and Payton sat on the far right end of the first row of seats. Gunter Wilke sat on the left aisle. I was surprised to see his son, Ernest, next to him. Maybe he wanted to be near Christabella in her moment of anguish. Hah!

I sat way off to the left, separated from the defense table only by a railing. On the right side of the courtroom was another table and State's Attorney Robert Velery was there, looking at a pile of documents. I had met Velery a number of times on other cases. He was a tiny man, barely five-feet-tall, and like most men that short, he was treacherous, nasty, and mean of spirit. An ideal prosecutor, in other words, and I liked to have him on my side when we were trying to nail somebody.

As I took my seat next to Patrolman Jackson, Drossner came down the center aisle of the courtroom, pushed open the swinging gate, and sat down next to Velery.

I glanced around the courtroom and saw Chief Semple sitting in the middle of the room next to Miss Milton, our First Selectperson. I looked away quickly before he could see me and bellow "Jezail!" in the crowded courtroom.

At precisely ten a.m., Alden Barkmore and Alfred Needles came into the courtroom through a side door. They were accompanied by a state trooper in full Smoky-the-Bear costume. Needles sat down at the defense table and the trooper sat in a chair behind him, against the railing. He was there to guard the prisoner and make sure he didn't escape.

Barkmore came over to the railing to me. I leaned forward.

"Did you see Leonardo yet?" I asked.

"I spoke to him on the telephone," he said.

"Will he be here?"

"He'd better. He's all I've got. Do you know what he's up to?"

I shook my head no and sat back in my seat. Barkmore nodded and went back to the counsel table. He was wearing a dark blue suit today with a white patterned shirt and red and blue regimental striped tie. His fingernails were manicured and he still smelled of lilac. I hoped he was a good lawyer. He sat next to Needles and put his arm around the man's shoulders, for solace. Maybe he was all right after all.

At four minutes after ten the bailiff entered and did his "Hear ye, hear ye" number and ordered us to rise. As we straggled to our feet, Judge Willis came in and took his seat on the bench, which was built on a raised platform so it dominated the courtroom with the feeling of the height and the majesty of the law. Just as it should be.

Behind me, reporters shuffled papers. Judge Willis said, "Please be seated."

He was a good judge, and he looked like a good judge, too. He had a full head of wavy gray hair, a stern, no-nonsense face, a voice that seemed to come from the pits of time, and a knowledge of the law that often shamed young prosecutors and defense attorneys who came before him unprepared. Needles would get a fair shake from him.

The bailiff announced, "The State of Connecticut versus Alfred Needles," and Willis asked, "Is Mr. Needles represented by counsel?"

Barkmore rose. "Mr. Needles is so represented, your honor. I am Alden Barkmore, attorney for the accused."

"Are you ready, Mr. Barkmore?"

"I am, your honor."

"Is the state ready?"

"Ready, your honor," Velery said, rising from the other table.

"Is your client ready to plead, Mr. Barkmore?"

"He is, sir."

"Mr. Needles, please rise," Judge Willis said.

Needles got slowly to his feet. Even from behind, without looking at his face, I could see he was still stunned by all this. His body looked disoriented, as if it were not obeying orders from his brain.

"Mister Needles, the charge is that you did willfully, maliciously, and feloniously take the life of one Barry Dawson in the town of Walton County of Fairfield, Connecticut. Do you understand the charge against you?"

Needles mumbled. Even from just a few feet away, I could not hear him.

"Mr. Barkmore," Judge Willis said.

"The defendant understands the charge, your honor," Barkmore said.

"And how does he plead?"

"Innocent," Needles said. "I am innocent."

"My client pleads not guilty," Barkmore corrected.

Innocent is a gray term that hasn't any place in a courtroom. The question is guilty or not guilty. They can find you not guilty without believing that you're innocent. Maybe you did it and the state just couldn't prove it. The jury knows that so they declare you not guilty. They don't declare you innocent. That's a job for God later on.

"Thank you. You may be seated."

Needles sat down. Barkmore remained standing.

"Mr. Barkmore, do you have a bail request?"

"May I approach the bench, your honor?"

"Please do."

Barkmore stopped five feet in front of the judge's bench.

"At this time, sir, the accused requests a full hearing in this matter," he said.

"That is most unusual, Mr. Barkmore. It is our general policy merely to accept a plea and to rule on a bail application."

"I understand that, your honor. However, we feel that Mr. Needles has been wrongly accused. And we request a prima facie hearing in the matter because we are prepared this morning not only to demonstrate that Mr. Needles is not guilty, but why he could not be. And this will afford the police time to apprehend the true murderer of Barry Dawson."

There was a buzz of voices in the courtroom. Velery leaned over to talk to Drossner.

Angrily, Judge Willis pounded his gavel. "I will at this time caution the spectators to remain silent," he intoned. "A press card gives no one the right to violate the order and decorum of this court."

Good for him.

The voices ceased immediately, but there was another sound in the back of the courtroom. The door opened and Leonardo came in, wearing a crisp gray pin-stripe suit, a gray shirt, and a red and gray tie. He looked like an advertisement from a fashion magazine, except for one thing. He was carrying a green plastic garbage bag at his side. It looked full.

Leonardo came down the center aisle through the gate and went to the counsel table where he sat alongside Barkmore's empty chair. He pushed the trash bag under the table, and nodded an apology to the judge for his lateness.

"Do you plan to call witnesses to this end, Mr. Barkmore?" the judge said.

"Yes, your honor."

"Your witnesses are in court?"

Barkmore glanced toward Leonardo, then with a smile told the judge, "Yes, your honor."

"And what is the state's position on this?" Willis asked Velery.

The small man got up. "We feel it is all unnecessary theatrics, your honor, and request the court to follow the normal procedure of arraignment."

"Surely, your honor," said Barkmore, "exposing the truth and clearing an innocent man is not considered unnecessary theatrics by the State's Attorney for Connecticut."

Willis paused for a moment, pondering. He finally nodded.

"We will allow you your opportunity, Mr. Barkmore. The aim of a court is to provide and dispense justice. In this complicated case, the dispensing of justice may mean the vigorous searching-out of the truth. The truth must have a higher priority than the precedents of custom and time. But I caution you. We are breaking new ground here and I will not hesitate to curtail these proceedings if I feel they are not productive or, are in any way, injurious to the best interests of the defendant. You may begin, Mister Velery."

Velery looked disgusted but called Patrolman Jackson who testified quickly and efficiently about how he was called to the Dawson studio by the telephone repairman, entered the building by breaking a window, discovered that Dawson was dead, and radioed for assistance.

Doc Spears was next. He testified that death was caused by a blow or blows to the side of the head, using a hammer that he identified. He said it was not necessarily so that Barry Dawson died instantly. He could have lived for a few minutes and yes, he might even have moved somewhat, crawling around the room. "The dying often have unusual powers," he said, "born of desperation."

Barkmore courteously declined any opportunity to question the state's witnesses. He and Leonardo seemed to be spending most of their time conferring over a long list written on a yellow legal pad.

Even from across the rail, I could spot Leonardo's crabbed handwriting, a kind of italic printing. Poor Needles just looked straight ahead, a man in a catatonic trance. If a bomb had been exploded in the courtroom, I don't think he would have moved a muscle.

And that damn plastic garbage bag sat under the counsel table, and I wondered just what kind of bag of tricks it was.

Velery's next witness was Inspector Drossner, filled with himself, good tailoring, and bright white teeth.

Under careful, methodical questioning from Velery, and using photographs that my man Daniels shot at the scene, he described the location of the body, the bloodstains, the key to the room, and how the door could only be locked from the inside. He identified the

diamond-studded tie-tack as the one that was found
in Dawson's hand. They could have called me to testify
to this, but I guess it would have cut into Drossner's
air time.

"To whom does the tie-tack belong?" Velery asked.

"To the defendant, Mr. Alfred Needles," Drossner
said.

"Did Mr. Needles tell you how that tie-tack came
to be in Barry Dawson's hand?"

"He said that it had been in his jewelry box in his
room and someone had taken it." Drossner's tone of
voice told clearly what he thought about *that*.

"Do you have a theory about what happened between four and seven p.m. on Thursday, April fifteenth, in the studio of Barry Dawson?"

The question raised hackles on my neck. Even a
cop can recognize an improper question. Judge Willis
looked toward the defense table and by reflex action,
Barkmore began to get to his feet to object. But he
was restrained by Leonardo who grabbed his forearm
and nodded to him.

"Please answer the question," Judge Willis finally
said.

"Yes, I do," said Drossner.

"Please explain your theory," Velery said.

"I believe that after Mr. Gunter Wilke, who was installing a kitchen, had left for the day, Mr. Dawson
left his office for a brief period of time. When he returned, he found someone burglarizing the office. If
you will recall from the photo entered into evidence,
the drawers of the chest showed signs of having been

ransacked. I believe Mr. Dawson struggled with the
burglar, who then struck him down with a hammer.
The burglar then took pains to conceal his identity.
First, he pressed Mr. Dawson's hand onto the handle
of the hammer in an unsuccessful attempt to confuse
the investigators. Then he fled, discarding the hammer
as he went. But Mr. Dawson was not yet dead. In the
struggle with his assailant, he had ripped the tie-tack
from the burglar's tie. He knew that it would be definitive proof of who had killed him and so, with his last
breaths, he crawled to the door and locked it, knowing that the tie-tack would be the evidence that would
bring his killer to justice."

"And that killer . . ."

"Is Mr. Alfred Needles, the owner of the tie-tack."

Needles seemed to wake up for a moment, about to
speak, to move, to do something, but Alden Barkmore
whispered something to him, and he sank back in his
seat.

"Now, Inspector Drossner," Velery asked, "why
would Alfred Needles burglarize his employer's studio?"

"We still hope to ascertain the answer to that question," Drossner said. "However, in a statement from
Mr. Barkmore, the defense counsel, it appeared that
Barry Dawson may have been contemplating changes
in his will, changes that might adversely have affected
Alfred Needles. He may have been looking for a draft
of a new will. He may have been looking for something altogether different. We do not know." Drossner
smiled with malicious glee. "It should not be over-

looked that Alfred Needles is a convicted burglar of long standing."

At the defense table, Leonardo and Barkmore looked up quickly. Drossner's words seemed like a hammer that crushed the final bit of spirit from Needles. He slumped forward and put his head on his arms.

Drossner was pulling a paper from his pocket.

"I have here a report from the Clark County Sheriff's office in Nevada. Mr. Alfred Needles was arrested there in 1958 on seventeen burglary charges and sentenced to serve three years in prison. After his parole, he went to work for Barry Dawson."

So that was it. Drossner's bombshell. I could hear the reporters buzzing behind me. They recognized something new when they heard it. Also, that frigging Drossner had probably told them all about it beforehand.

Velery took the paper and handed it to Judge Willis, then went back to stand again in front of Drossner.

"Will any other set of circumstances satisfy the facts in this case? Specifically, the locked door, the murder weapon with the victim's fingerprints on it, the tietack found in Barry Dawson's hand?"

"None that I can discern," said Drossner. "I think in death, Barry Dawson composed the greatest, most meaningful riddle of his life. And I think we solved it."

The bastard. He had probably sat up all night writing that little speech. He would do anything to get into the papers.

"Those are all my questions. Your honor. I think we have shown clearly here enough evidence to hold this man over for trial."

"Not quite so fast, Mr. Velery," Judge Willis said. "Mr. Barkmore, have you any questions of this witness?"

"No, your honor," Barkmore said, slowly rising.

"Do you intend to call witnesses?"

"Just one, your honor."

"Please proceed," Willis said. "You are excused, Inspector."

Jauntily, Drossner hopped down from the witness stand. He could not resist a slight sneer in Leonardo's direction as he went back to his seat at the prosecution table.

Barkmore said: "I call David Vincent Leonardo."

CHAPTER FOURTEEN

"Your full name, please."

"David Vincent Leonardo."

"What is your occupation?"

"I am a professor of mathematics at Misericordia College."

"And you hold academic degrees?"

"Yes."

"What are they, please?"

"I hold doctorates in mathematics, philosophy, and anthropology. I have a degree in psychoanalytic practice from the University of Bern in Switzerland. I have several other degrees."

Velery rose. "Doctor Leonardo's credentials as a scholar are well-known to most of us. It is his credentials in the Dawson case that I am not quite sure of."

"Thank you for reminding me," Leonardo said to Velery. "I hold a degree in forensic medicine from the

Sorbonne and in criminology from the University of Tubingen." He paused. "In addition, I am a special consultant to the Walton Police Department."

He looked at Velery who lifted a hand in disgusted surrender. The spectators in the courtroom tittered a little but Judge Willis was smiling too, so he did not chew them out.

"And it was in your function as special consultant to the Walton Police that you first became involved in the case of Barry Dawson, is that correct?" asked Barkmore.

"It is."

"You have heard Inspector Drossner's theory of how this crime took place. What is your opinion of that theory?"

"It is highly ingenious," Leonardo said. "However, it is fallacious in the extreme. Ingenuity has never been an acceptable substitute for correctness in such matters."

"Do you have a theory of your own on this crime?"

"I object, your honor," Velery said quickly.

"Judge," said Barkmore, "we are merely following along the path first carved by Mr. Velery himself. It was he who introduced Inspector Drossner's theorizing into this hearing. We must have the right to respond to that."

Judge Willis looked at Velery with sympathy. "I'm afraid, Mr. Velery, that you have been euchred. Please sit down. Continue, Mr. Barkmore."

Barkmore went back to the counsel table to pick up

the yellow pad over which he and Leonardo had been conferring. "Shall I repeat the question, Doctor?"

"That will not be necessary," Leonardo said. "You asked if I had a theory of my own on the Dawson crime. I have more than a theory. I have facts."

"And what is the substance of those facts?"

"That Mr. Alfred Needles did not kill Barry Dawson."

There was a collective sip of air in the courtroom, as if the building itself were inhaling.

"Can you prove that?"

"The proof that something did not happen is very difficult," Leonardo said. "However, I can demonstrate it with more surety than Inspector Drossner attempted to prove that Mr. Needles *did* commit the murder."

Barkmore could not resist turning and glancing toward Velery. "As a doctor in forensic medicine and as a doctor of criminology and as a special consultant to the Walton Police Department, would you please analyze the case for us and give us some of your conclusions on the matter?"

"I should be glad to," Leonardo said.

Barkmore went back and leaned against the defense table while Leonardo talked. Alfred Needles kept looking down, as if watching a fleas' football game being played on the table.

"There are a number of aspects of the case against Alfred Needles and it might be helpful to take them in order," Leonardo said.

"First, the diamond tie-tack. There is no question

that it belongs to Mr. Needles. That is admitted by the accused. Needles said he lost the clip that fastens the tie-tack and so put the tie-tack into the jewelry box on his dresser until he could secure another clip for it. The state chooses not to believe this explanation. However, the state does not answer the question that must then be raised. Where is the clip that held the tie-tack?"

He looked around the courtroom with that vacant bemused glance I had often seen him adopt before his classes during a lecture.

"If the tie-tack had been ripped off in a struggle, the clip should have fallen to the floor. But it was not on the floor of Barry Dawson's office. Nor was it outside the door, nor was it on the path leading to the Dawson house. Perhaps Alfred Needles picked it up himself? That would be senseless. Why would he pick up the clip from the studio floor and leave the tie-tack, the evidence, in Mr. Dawson's clenched hand? On Friday, when Inspector Drossner, Lieutenant Jezail of the Walton Police, and I went to the main Dawson house, I took the opportunity to search the clothing Alfred Needles had worn on the night of the Dawson murder on the chance that the clip might have fallen into a pocket or a cuff. There was no clip to be found in his clothing.

"Rather than concoct a fanciful theory that strains to cover the known facts, how much simpler to take Mr. Needles's word at face value. The ties tack was in his jewelry box because he had lost the clip to it. And someone removed it from the jewelry box and put it in

Barry Dawson's hand in order to fix the blame for Dawson's murder on Alfred Needles."

Leonardo paused to take a drink of water from the plastic mug on the side of the witness box.

"Then there are the twin questions of time and the tuning of the color television set. Doctor Spears has fixed the hour of Barry Dawson's death at between four and seven p.m. But at 6 p.m., Alfred Needles was in his room at the main house, accepting delivery of a color television set. This has been confirmed to me by the installation man. Mr. Needles said that shortly after seven p.m., he ate dinner at the Golden Palace Restaurant. This is confirmed by those who work in the restaurant.

"That sequence leaves Alfred Needles precious little time to have murdered his employer between six and seven p.m. And to have burglarized the studio. And to have devised a method of locking the door behind himself.

"Mr. Needles tuned the television himself after the installation man left. Lieutenant Jezail and I examined the television set and the lieutenant will confirm that the picture had a decidedly bluish cast. Recent studies have correlated the way a person tints a color television set with the person's frame of mind at that time. It is agreed that a set tuned toward the blue color reflects a person who is generally placid and tranquil. We should hardly expect Mr. Needles to be in that frame of mind after having killed his employer and friend, unless of course he was deliriously happy over the thought of a meal of Szechuan shredded beef."

Drossner had been trying to look bored through Leonardo's statement but now he was beginning to get annoyed. His neck was turning red and I wanted to tell him that it was a bad contrast to the television-blue collar of his shirt. Leonardo, on the other hand, looked as placid as if he had just awakened from a three-month sleep.

"And there is the matter of the hammer, the death weapon. According to Inspector Drossner, Mr. Needles was surprised in the act of the burglary, fought with Dawson, and struck him down. However, Mr. Wilke has told police that the hammer was taken from his tool box, which was stored in another part of the studio building. How then did it come so conveniently to hand to serve as a weapon for Alfred Needles's murderous act of passion? But let that go for a moment.

"Why, we must ask, did Needles put Dawson's fingerprints on the hammer? Why did he discard it along the path near the house when with a little extra effort he could have thrown it into the furze that grows a few hundred feet away and where it might never have been found? Why would he discard it along the path in the direction of the main house, knowing that would inevitably throw suspicion on someone in the main house? Such as himself.

"Again, how much simpler to believe the obvious solution. The hammer was used to throw suspicion on someone in the main house. It was left near the path by someone clever and crafty. And malicious, because putting Mr. Dawson's fingerprints on the hammer was done merely to confound the police and to intensify the riddle.

"And now we have the question of Mr. Dawson's supposed action in crawling to the door to lock the door, then crawling back into the room to die, all in order to create an airtight case against Mr. Needles. I suggest that that is absurd. *De mortuis nil nisi bonum.* We should speak nothing but well of the dead. Still there is nothing in Barry Dawson's books to indicate he had such logical skills of mind to do such a thing.

"Yet, suppose he had his wits about him. He knew he was dying. He wanted to name his murderer. Why did this man of words not simply crawl to his desk and with his Bic pen and yellow legal pad write 'Needles killed me.' From the start, there has been no reason why Barry Dawson would act the way Inspector Drossner surmises he acted."

He took another sip of water. "And finally there is the point of the burglarized cabinet. May I have the photograph, your honor?"

Judge Willis had been listening to Leonardo's testimony intently, obviously impressed. It took him a split-second to remember he was the judge and not just another spectator, and he rummaged through the exhibits on the desk in front of him and handed Leonardo the photo Daniels had taken of the cabinet.

Leonardo looked at it and said, "Inspector Drossner has made much of the fact that in the long ago past Alfred Needles was a burglar. If you will look at this photograph of the cabinet that was apparently burglarized, you will note that the cabinet has four drawers on each side. The top three on either side were almost closed. The bottom one on each side remained open. This means that the burglar, if there was a burglar, opened the top drawer, rummaged through it, closed it, then opened the next one down, and so forth, until he reached the bottom one, which he left open. He did the same on both sides of the cabinet.

"I suggest, Mr. Barkmore, that the fact of Alfred Needles's record of burglary, rather than throw guilt on him, helps indicate his innocence. It is well known among policemen that professional burglars have devised certain efficient patterns of operation. For instance, no professional burglar would start searching a cabinet by working from the top down. He would start at the bottom drawers and work up. This way he does not have to close the drawers he has already opened and ransacked. This method saves time, and time is generally crucial to burglars—most especially, it would seem, to burglars who are looting their employer's office in mid-day, expecting him to return at any moment, and who are in a hurry besides to get to a Chinese restaurant for dinner."

Needles nodded agreement; he was finally coming alive. There was a faint snicker of laughter in the back of the room and Judge Willis looked up with an angry glare that could have shattered glass.

Leonardo handed the photograph back to the judge.

"These facts about burglars and their methods are, by the way, contained in *Tools of the Trade*, Barry Dawson's first book, which was written in 1958 and 1959 when Mr. Dawson was living in Clark County, Nevada, awaiting a divorce from the first Mrs. Dawson. I suspect that his technical adviser on that book was Alfred Needles and that Barry Dawson's subsequent offer of employment to Needles hastened his parole from prison. The 'threat' that Barry Dawson considered Alfred Needles's burglary record is perhaps shown in the dedication of *Pieces of Eight*, Mr. Dawson's last book. It reads 'For a lousy burglar and a great friend.' So much for any animosity between them that might have impelled Barry Dawson to cut Needles from his will. And so much for the case against Alfred Needles. The case is nonexistent. Mr. Needles did not kill Barry Dawson."

Angry, because he spoke without rising, Velery snarled toward Leonardo, "And I guess you can tell us who did kill Dawson?"

"Of course I can," said Leonardo coolly.

"Control yourself, Mr. Velery," Judge Willis said. "Continue, Doctor."

"Thank you, Judge. A few preliminary points. Christabella Dawson told police that she had argued with her husband at the gate on the steps between the main house and the studio. He then slapped her. Gunter Wilke confirmed that they talked at the gate. He said he was working alone on the kitchen of the Dawson studio.

"However, Mrs. Dawson told Inspector Drossner

that when she approached the gate she heard the
sound of work*men*. Plural. She said specifically that
she heard the sound of hammering and the sound of
an electric saw at the same time. I doubt that even so
good a workman as Gunter Wilke was able to operate
both a hammer and electric saw at the same time. So
why did he tell us he was working alone? A minor
point but perhaps significant.

"Mr. Wilke also did not mention his son, Ernest.
But the business is Wilke and Son, and when Lieutenant Jezail and I met Ernest Wilke yesterday, his father was quick to say that the son had been ill and
presumably off the job. It appeared that Gunter Wilke
did not want his son's name to be connected in any
way with Thursday's events at the Dawson studio.

"Gunter Wilke, on another occasion, told police
that he always walked down to the beach to eat his
lunch. But yesterday, when we met his son at the work
site, Gunter Wilke declined to leave and, instead, remained inside the building to eat his lunch. Again a
minor point by itself, but again, perhaps significant.
He did not want to leave his son alone with us."

"Does this have a point, Doctor?" asked Judge
Willis.

"It does, Your Honor. What Gunter Wilke did not
want us to find out was that Ernest Wilkie, his son,
is Christabella Dawson's lover."

There was noise in the courtroom. I turned to
watch Christabella look down the bench in panic at
young Ernie. He did not look at her. His thick lips
now didn't appear sensuous; they looked pouting, as if

about to cry. Old man Wilke sat next to him, stone-still, no expression on his face.

"Lieutenant Jezail and I ascertained this last night at a New York City restaurant where Mrs. Dawson and young Mr. Wilke had dined on Thursday night, the night of Mr. Dawson's murder, and by checking the registry of a nearby hotel where they checked in as man and wife and spent the night. A clerk will identify them. This is in direct contradiction to what Mrs. Dawson told Lieutenant Jezail about where she had spent Thursday night.

"Yesterday, when we met Ernest Wilke at the studio, he kept checking his watch as if he had an appointment. A few moments after he left, Christabella Dawson came to the studio fence as if to meet someone. But young Wilke had already gone and when she saw us, she turned back and returned to the house.

"What I suggest now is only hypothesis. Mrs. Dawson argued with her husband, and Ernest Wilke, working in the studio at the time, saw and/or heard them. Sometime after Mr. Dawson slapped her, Ernest Wilke argued with him about this treatment of Christabella. Perhaps at this time, Barry Dawson already knew of his wife's infidelity. Perhaps that was behind his decision to change his will, to remove Christabella. At any rate, Ernest and Dawson argued, and in a rage, Ernest Wilke struck down Barry Dawson with the hammer he held in his hand."

Leonardo stopped to take his eyeglasses from his inside jacket pocket. He began to chew on the earpiece.

"Gunter Wilke had seen what had happened but it had occurred too quickly for him to prevent it. Now this loving father knows what will happen. His son will be arrested for murder. He will go to jail. But there is still a chance. He tells his son to go home and that his story will be that he has been ill and in bed. No one, remember, had seen Ernest Wilke on Thursday at the work site. Young Wilke left, but could not resist keeping his appointment with Christabella that night in New York City. Perhaps there he told her what he had done. Perhaps he did not tell her. Perhaps she already knew because this had been a plan of theirs for some time. I do not know the answer to that.

"Meanwhile, Gunter Wilke began to calculate a plan to protect his son by throwing suspicion on others. It was he who pulled out the drawers in the chest. It was he who put Dawson's prints on the hammer and discarded it along the path to the main house. It was he who went up to the main house to find incriminating evidence. He waited until it was dark before going up. He had to be careful that the gate to the main house did not lock behind him, so he tied it open with a yellow wire tie, the kind used to fasten garbage bags. This is it here."

From a jacket pocket, Leonardo took the wire tie. It was what I'd thought was a yellow strip of paper on Friday. He handed it to the judge.

"I am sorry for its condition, sir," he told Judge Willis, "but it was damaged when Inspector Drossner stepped on it Friday while we were walking to the

Dawson house. The tie is, by the way, identical to the kind that Mr. Wilke uses to fasten his sandwich bags for lunch. Lieutenant Jezail and I noticed this yesterday.

"To continue. Gunter Wilke got to the main house and found it empty. He went to Mr. Needles's room and stole the tie-tack to leave in the dead Mr. Dawson's hand." Leonardo's voice suddenly got louder as he called out, "Mr. Needles?"

Needles looked up.

"Who built the bookshelves in your room?"

Needles seemed confused for a moment, then said, "Gunter Wilke."

"Thank you," Leonardo said. "Gunter Wilke had ample opportunity while doing that carpentry work to notice Alfred Needles's jewelry box on his dresser. Perhaps once he even looked inside. When he needed an incriminating piece of evidence, he had a good idea of where to look. Perhaps he bore no animosity to Alfred Needles but that did not matter. His son's very life was at stake."

He paused. Slightly turned in my seat, I could see the elder Wilke gesture contemptuously at Leonardo, dismissing everything he had said.

"Then he hurried back to the studio. When he pulled the gate closed behind him, perhaps he could not find the piece of yellow wire in the dark. Perhaps he just forgot it. At any rate, he left it lying there. And he went back to Dawson's room, put the tie-tack in Barry Dawson's hand, and when he was done, he went home."

Leonardo raised his hands in front of him, palms up, signifying "and that was that."

"Thank you, Doctor," said Barkmore. Velery was on his feet.

"May I, your honor?"

"Go ahead," Judge Willis said.

"You seem to have thought of everything, Doctor Leonardo, except the locked room. How did Gunter Wilke, in this fanciful invention of yours, lock the door from the inside when he left? How was it that the key to the room was found in Barry Dawson's hand? Behind a locked door? How?"

"Very simple," Leonardo said. He motioned to me. "Lieutenant Jezail, have you that poem?"

I took the sheet of yellow paper from the pocket of my jacket, and gave it to the bailiff. He carried it up to the judge who glanced at it and handed it to Leonardo.

"This was the top sheet from a tablet on Barry Dawson's desk," said Leonardo. "The handwriting has been verified as his by Mr. Barkmore, his attorney and agent. It is dated, by Barry Dawson himself, on April fifteenth, the day of his death. May I read this, Judge?"

He looked to Willis, who seemed to be enjoying himself. "I don't think I could stop you now if I wanted to," he said. "Go ahead."

Leonardo cleared his throat and began to read:

April Fifteenth.
The sun lives and creates life.

Master builder, it rides high and golden
and turns the dull brown of dirt
into the brightness of flowered fields.
The sun dies and creates death,
but in an imitation of life.
The red ball sends its rays
through colored glass,
splashing dagger-jagging flashes
of colored lights against dirt-colored
oaken panels that once also lived.
The sun's life is the color of gold.
The sun's death is the color of blood.
The sun is just like man.

When he was finished, he looked up but no one in the court seemed to understand the significance of the poem.

"Very nice," sneered Velery. "But what does that have to do with anything?"

"It is obviously a poem that Mr. Barry Dawson wrote while he was watching the dying sun of late afternoon, flashing in through the stained glass panels over and around the front door of his studio building."

"So what?" asked Velery.

"So Gunter Wilke told Inspector Drossner and Lieutenant Jezail, in a statement, that Barry Dawson had kept the door to his office closed all day."

"And?" asked Velery.

"The question is how did Mr. Barry Dawson see the dying sun of late afternoon when there was a wall between his desk and the glass panels at the end of the building?"

Gunter Wilke rose to his feet and shook his right index finger at Leonardo.

"Damn you. Damn you. Damn you."

"Be silent," Judge Willis shouted again. "Damn you."

"Bailiff, restrain that man," Willis said.

Gunter Wilke stood in his place defiantly. His son buried his face in his hands. Christabella Dawson wept loudly.

Two Walton policemen came to the ends of the row of seats where the Wilkes sat and stood there ominously.

Leonardo continued as if there had been no interruption at all.

"Barry Dawson's body was found in a locked room, yes. But the fact is that the room was built only after he was dead. Gunter Wilke built the final wall after the murder to pose the puzzle for police. Perhaps he suffered pangs of conscience. Perhaps he wanted to make it more difficult for the police to arrest Alfred Needles. For whatever reason, he built the wall only after his son had killed Barry Dawson. He built the entire wall, save one panel section at the end. Inside the almost-built room, he moved the body of Barry Dawson around to create blood stains and smears. He put Barry Dawson's bloodied hand on the doorknob to leave traces there. He put the key to the room and the tie-tack in the dead man's hand. Then he stepped outside the room, and simply nailed into place the final panel that completed the room. The rug that covers the entire floor of the studio building passes under that wall. The wall was erected after the rug was laid."

"You bastard," Gunter Wilke shouted.

"Mr. Velery. Inspector Drossner. I suggest that you take these people into custody while you determine exactly what charges are to be filed against whom."

"Yes, your honor," Velery said. Drossner stood and motioned to his men in the back of the room. They came forward quickly and led the Wilkes and Christabella Dawson from the courtroom, which quickly broke into pandemonium. Reporters were running around, back and forth, confused, not knowing whom to talk to, so they talked to each other. Photographers pushed into the back swinging doors to photograph the Wilkes and Christabella being taken into custody.

The confusion had finally triggered him into action and Chief Semple was going for his gun. He probably thought he had a full-blown press riot on his hands.

"Will everybody please take his seat?" Judge Willis said. "This court has not been adjourned."

Slowly, order returned to the courtroom. When it was again quiet, the judge looked over at Leonardo.

"Doctor," he said, "you *are* going to tell us what is in that garbage bag you dragged into court, are you not?"

"Yes sir. I had almost forgotten. While Lieutenant Jezail and I were with the Wilkes at the Dawson studio yesterday, Gunter Wilke insisted that his son remove the tarpaulin that he used as a painting drop cloth. I thought this was somewhat unusual since there was more painting work to be done over the sink. But I thought nothing more of it until this morning, when I realized the significance of that tarpaulin.

"When he was in the studio with the dead Barry Dawson and he hit upon his bizarre plan to build the final office wall, Gunter Wilke was faced with a problem. He could not just leave the body of Barry Dawson lying on the floor while he built the wall. Somebody might come to the studio. Anyone could come down from the parking lot. So he covered the body with the tarpaulin, to hide it from view.

"When he was done, he folded it up and put it back near the sink for later use. But he must have thought about it and reconsidered because this was why he came back on Saturday, allegedly to work. He wanted the tarpaulin removed. His son carried it up and put it into the back of the Wilkes's work truck.

"This morning I realized what that tarpaulin must have been used for. I waited until I was sure the Wilkes were both in court, and I went to their home. I found the tarpaulin in their garage. That is it in the bag. It has bloodstains on it, and I am sure they will match the blood type of Barry Dawson."

"Thank you, Doctor," Judge Willis said. "Mister Velery, have you any objection to the dismissal of the charge against Alfred Needles?"

"No, your honor."

"Fine. It is done. Our thanks, Professor, for a most enlightening morning. Court is adjourned."

This time the courtroom really went wild as reporters scurried out looking for the nearest telephones.

Barkmore helped Needles to his feet.

"It's all over?" Needles asked, a pathetic, lost tone in his voice.

"Yes," said Barkmore.

Needles sighed deeply. Leonardo came down from the witness box and joined them as I walked up. He nodded toward Inspector Drossner, then to me.

Reporters came pressing down the aisle toward Leonardo and he said, "Let us get out of here. I hate mob scenes."

"Keep them away," I told the state trooper who had been sitting behind Needles. He nodded and blocked the gate so the reporters couldn't follow us.

Leonardo and I walked after Barkmore and Needles out the side door to the empty prisoners' waiting room.

I lit a cigarette for myself and Leonardo asked for one, too. We smoked quietly, while we waited for the crowd noises outside to calm down.

"All right, wise guy," I said. "How did you know that was the way it was?"

"The rip in your jacket," Leonardo said. "We both saw how meticulous a craftsman Gunter Wilke is. Yet you ripped your jacket on a nail near the door. None of the nails in that wall had been covered over with paint or a putty stick when we first went there. This morning they were all covered, so Gunter Wilke must have done that yesterday after we left. It was unthinkable that under normal circumstances he would have forgotten to cover over the finishing nails. Unless he was racing against time to build a wall quickly. The jacket was my first suspicion. It was confirmed when I read Mr. Dawson's poem."

"Incredible," said Alden Barkmore. "Quite a display."

"Nothing really exceptional," Leonardo said. "It primarily involved keeping one's eyes open."

"And a knowledge of psychology, times of sunset, burglars' working habits, the ability to draw portraits, knowing how carpenters work, picking up the right piece of wire off the ground, and a half-dozen other things all filtered through a tight, logical net," I said. "Nothing, exceptional, huh?"

"All those things you mention," Leonardo said, "they are all part of the province of men's lives. Therefore if we would know why men do what men do, we must turn our back on nothing. All knowledge is relevant because all knowledge is part of the whole. Consistency may be the hobgoblin of small minds, but specialization is the ruination of all minds."

He looked up as he so often did in his classroom, to be sure we had heard and understood.

"Let that be a law by which you live," he said.

I nodded. "Leonardo's Law," I said.

EPILOGUE

Inspector Drossner had returned to Bridgeport to lick his wounds.

Chief Semple was mad at me, because I hadn't tipped him off that the Wilkes had done it so he could leak it to the press and get some good publicity for the good old Walton P.D.

First Selectperson Milton was quite happy that she had had the foresight to tell me to bring Leonardo into the case, and she would not be hurt if I managed to mention that to some of the reporters who would be interviewing me in the future.

It was all right. None of those things could bother me today.

And then I went home. Adele was sleeping on the couch. There was half a martini in a glass on the floor.

I tried to wake her.

"We cleared him," I said.

"Who?"

"Needles. He didn't do it."

"Who did?" she asked thickly.

"The Wilkes. The builders."

"Too bad," she said. "I was hoping it was you."

I left the house. Later that afternoon, I picked up Alfred Needles, Alden Barkmore, and Walter Payton at the Dawson house to drive them to Leonardo's for a drink.

When we arrived, Leonardo was again working on that infernal mouth but he put his paints away and mixed us all drinks.

We toasted Alfred Needles who seemed to have come almost all the way back to life.

"I want to thank you Professor," he said. "I was at the point where I thought we'd have to wait for Barry's soul to come back before we learned the truth."

Leonardo shook his head. "Too soon for that," he said. "He had not enough karma."

"Karma? Oh, *come*, Doctor," said Barkmore. "Surely, *you* don't believe in that stuff. Reincarnation. That people come back. You don't think that happens, do you?"

Leonardo smiled. "I *know* it happens," he said.

They talked on like that, about reincarnation and all that nonsense about people returning after death to live new lives, but I have to admit, I wasn't really paying too much attention.

I just couldn't get my eyes off that mouth on the wall.

I had seen it someplace before and someday I'd remember where.

ABOUT THE AUTHOR

Warren B. Murphy has written over three dozen published books, including THE RAZONI AND JACKSON DETECTIVE SERIES and THE DESTROYER series.

Both series have received vast critical acclaim. THE DESTROYER, which Mr. Murphy co-authors with Richard Sapir, has been given an excellent rating by *The New York Times* and other prestigious publications.

Mr. Murphy has been a newspaperman, campaign consultant, and politician. He has also written for Warner Brothers and for Universal Pictures. He is an active member of the western division of the Writers Guild of America and the Author's League of America.

Occasionally married, Mr. Murphy pursues many hobbies including chess, mathematics, puzzles, the martial arts and uphill skiing.

FREE!!
BOOKS BY MAIL
CATALOGUE

BOOKS BY MAIL will share with you our current bestselling books as well as hard to find specialty titles in areas that will match your interests. You will be updated on what's new in books at no cost to you. Just fill in the coupon below and discover the convenience of having books delivered to your home.

PLEASE ADD $1.00 TO COVER THE COST OF POSTAGE & HANDLING.

BOOKS BY MAIL
320 Steelcase Road E.,
Markham, Ontario L3R 2M1

IN THE U.S. -
210 5th Ave., 7th Floor
New York, N.Y., 10010

Please send Books By Mail catalogue to:

Name _____
(please print)

Address _____

City _____

Prov./State _____ P.C./Zip _____

(BBM1)